WILLIAM

SHAKESPEARE'S

THE

EMPIRE STRIKETH BACK

STAR WARS

PART THE FIFTH

WILLIAM

SHAKESPEARE'S

—— THE ——
EMPIRE STRIKETH BACK

STAR WARS

PART THE FIFTH

By Ian Doescher

INSPIRED BY THE WORK OF GEORGE LUCAS
AND WILLIAM SHAKESPEARE

QUIRK BOOKS
PHILADELPHIA

Library of Congress Cataloging in Publication Number: 2013913273

ISBN: 978-1-59474-715-1

Printed in the United States of America

Typeset in Sabon

Designed by Gregg Kulick
Text by Ian Doescher
Illustrations by Nicolas Delort
Production management by John J. McGurk

Quirk Books
215 Church Street
Philadelphia, PA 19106
quirkbooks.com

10 9 8 7 6 5 4 3 2 1

DRAMATIS PERSONAE

CHORUS

LUKE SKYWALKER, *a Jedi trainee*
GHOST OF OBI-WAN KENOBI, *a Jedi Knight*
YODA, *a Jedi Master*
PRINCESS LEIA ORGANA, *of Alderaan*
HAN SOLO, *a rebel captain*
CHEWBACCA, *his Wookiee and first mate*
C-3PO, *a droid*
R2-D2, *his companion*
LANDO OF CALRISSIAN, *a scoundrel*
LOBOT, *his man-at-arms*
GENERAL RIEEKAN, *of the Rebellion*
WEDGE ANTILLES, *a rebel pilot*
DACK, DERLIN, HOBBIE, JANSON, *and* ZEV, *soldiers of the Rebellion*
EMPEROR PALPATINE, *ruler of the Empire*
DARTH VADER, *a Sith Lord*
PIETT, OZZEL, VEERS, *and* NEEDA, *gentlemen of the Empire*
BOBA FETT, *a bounty hunter*
WAMPA ICE CREATURE, *of Hoth*
EXOGORTH, *of the asteroid field*
UGNAUGHTS, *merry dwarves of Bespin*

REBEL PILOTS, LIEUTENANTS, CONTROLLERS, AIDES,
DROIDS, BOUNTY HUNTERS, AT-ATS, IMPERIAL TROOPS,
OFFICERS, GUARDS, *and* SOLDIERS

PROLOGUE.

Outer space.

Enter CHORUS.

CHORUS   O, 'tis for the Rebellion a dark time.
For though they have the Death Star all destroy'd,
Imperi'l troops did from the ashes climb
And push the rebels closer to the void.
Across the galaxy pursu'd with speed,   5
The rebels flee th'Imperi'l Starfleet vast.
A group with Luke Skywalker in the lead
Hath to the ice world known as Hoth flown fast.
Meanwhile, the cruel Darth Vader is obsess'd
With finding young Skywalker. Thus he hath   10
Through ev'ry point of space begun his quest
By sending robot probes to aid his wrath.
In time so long ago begins our play,
In war-torn galaxy far, far away.
                                      [Exit.

ACT I

SCENE 1.

The ice world of Hoth.

Enter LUKE SKYWALKER.

LUKE   If flurries be the food of quests, snow on.
Belike upon this Hoth, this barren rock,
My next adventure waits. 'Tis time shall tell.
And yet, is it adventure that I seek?
Shall danger, fear, and action fill my days?   5
Shall all my life be spent in keen pursuit
Of great adventure and her fickle fame?
It seemeth I have had enough of life
To fill a thousand normal human lives—
A princess in a vision spake to me,   10
My aunt and uncle by stormtroopers slain,
A hasty flight from my home, Tatooine,
A pilot and a Wookiee and a Knight,
A rescue brave within our cruel foe's grasp,
My teacher kill'd, and then the final scene: 15
The Death Star battle—many friends were lost,
But in the end a greater war was won.
Adventure hath both taken from my life,
And given to me ev'rything I have.
And thus I seek and shun its tempting ways.   20
E'en now adventure knocks upon the door:
A flaming orb hath struck the ground nearby.
Is it a portent of some ill to come?
[*Into comlink:*] 'Tis Echo-Three to
                 Echo-Seven: Han,

	My true companion e'er, canst thou hear me?	25
HAN	[*through comlink:*] Aye, truly, chuck, thy voice	
	rings loud and clear.	
	What can I do for thee, my noble friend?	
LUKE	My circle 'round the area hath been	
	Completed now, but naught of life nor forms	
	Of life my scan hath yet uncover'd.	
HAN	[*through comlink:*] —Nay.	30
	There is not life enough upon this cube	
	Of ice to fill an empty space cruiser.	
	The sensors have I put in place, so shall	
	I now return unto the base.	
LUKE	—'Tis well,	
	And I, forsooth, shall soon meet with thee there.	35
	But I have spied a met'orite that hath	
	Its landing made near here. So shall I go	

And fix my eyes upon the scene. I'll not
Be long, I warrant; then, I shall return.

Enter WAMPA, *aside.*

WAMPA   You viewers all, whose gentle hearts do fear   40
         The smallest womp rat creeping on the floor,
         May now perchance both quake and tremble here,
         When wampa rough in wildest rage doth roar.
         Pray know that I a wampa simple am,
         And take no pleasure in my angry mood.   45
         Though with great force this young one's face I slam,
         I prithee know I strike but for my food.
LUKE   Alas, is this th'adventure I am due,
         To die upon a vicious monster's whim?
         I am attackèd by this awful beast!   50
         O fate most wretched—shall I be his feast?
                           [Exit, pursued by a wampa.

SCENE 2.

The rebel base on Hoth.

Enter HAN SOLO.

HAN   A scoundrel may not rise above his place—
         This is a fact the galaxy doth teach.
         For e'en though I have join'd rebellion's ranks
         These many weeks and months, and gain'd respect
         Within their noble band, my scoundrel past   5
         Doth make its harsh demands upon my life.

The bounty hunters sent by Jabba make
Pursuit to win the price upon my head.
So must I go once more unto the depths
Of my old life, find Jabba of the Hutt   10
And pay his ransom, thus to free my soul.
I would not leave my noble rebel friends,
I would not leave the cause for which they fight,
I would not leave the princess and her charm,
I would not leave all these, and yet I must.   15
A life's not well lived under threat of death,
Especially with men of cruel intent—
Who for a price shall fill the Hutt's demands—
Upon the trail of my indebtedness.
And so, my mate Chewbacca and I leave   20
Upon the instant that the ship is set to go.

Enter CHEWBACCA, *working on the* Millennium Falcon.

        I say, Chewbacca, ho! Aye, Chewie!

CHEWBAC.   —Auugh!

HAN   Lose not thy temper, gentle Wookiee, nay,
        But practice patience; I shall help thee soon.

CHEWBAC.   Egh, auugh, egh.

        [Exit Chewbacca. Han crosses to command center
             with Princess Leia and General Rieekan.

RIEEKAN   —Solo, wouldst thou speak with me?   25

HAN   Good general, the sensors are in place,
        And surely shalt thou know if aught comes near
        Our hidden station here.

RIEEKAN   —Well. Prithee say,
        Commander Skywalker, hath he yet made

Report?

HAN   —Nay, truly. He hath gone to see   30
                   A met'orite that hath made landfall near.

RIEEKAN   With all the met'orites a'falling in
                   This system, I believe we shall have pains
                   And trouble in detecting 'proaching ships.

HAN   [*aside:*] How shall I tell my news most difficult,   35
                   And crush this man's great hopes for what's ahead?
                   Fear not, O heart, but be direct and calm:
                   'Tis best approach'd straight on, like th'Kessel Run.
                   [*To Rieekan:*] My general, I cannot stay. I must
                   Make haste and get me hence, e'en now.

LEIA   [*aside:*]   —Alack,   40
                   How like a death knell sounds this news to me!

RIEEKAN   I tell thee truly when I say to thee:
                   This news doth break this gen'ral's gentle soul.
                   I could not be more sorry, pilot brave.

HAN   A price still lies upon my head, and if   45
                   I do not make amends with Jabba, I
                   Shall not repay with money, nay, but life.

RIEEKAN   A price too dear, indeed! A death mark is
                   No kind companion to a free man's life.
                   Thou art a warrior noble, Solo, and   50
                   I hate to lose thee.

HAN   —And thou art a kind,
                   Good general, sirrah, I hate to go.
                                     [*Exit Rieekan. Han turns to Princess Leia.*
                   And so, Your Highness great, this is the end.

LEIA   'Tis so.

HAN   —I prithee mourn me not, and show
                   No sentiment. Farewell, thou princess cold.   55

[*Aside:*] I go, and hope she'll follow hard upon,
For if she shall not follow, all is lost.

      [*Han Solo begins to exit, pursued by Princess Leia.*

LEIA   Han, halt!

HAN   —What is thy pleasure, Highness?

LEIA   I did believe that thou had chos'n to stay.

HAN   The bounty hunter we did meet on Ord   60
Mantell hath chang'd my mind.

LEIA   —We need thee, Han.

HAN   What "we"? Why speakest thou of "we"?
Dost thou in royal terms speak here of "we"?
Hast thou a rodent in thy pocket, such
That thou and he are "we"? What meanest thou?   65
What need is there that thou dost share with all?
Speak not of "we," but "I." O princess, what
Dost thou most need? Not "we," not "they," but thou?

LEIA   I know not what thou speakest of.

HAN   —'Tis true.
Most probably thou dost not know thyself.   70

LEIA   And what, pray tell, precisely should I know?
Of what great myst'ry am I unaware?
Hast thou the depths of Leia plumb'd and seen
What lies within my soul, my very core?

HAN   Be not elusive, nay! Thou wouldst that I   75
Should stay because of how thou feelest in
Thy heart about me. Need hath turn'd to want.
Pray, tell me not thy needs, but thy desires.

LEIA   Thou art a leader full of skill, 'tis true.

HAN   Thine answer leadeth thee astray. Let fly!   80
I see it in thine aspect now, let fly!
Tell me the answer true.

LEIA   —Thy vanity
          Hath puff'd up thine imagination.
HAN   —Aye?
          Then why dost thou yet follow me? Wert thou
          Afraid I would depart without a kiss?   85
LEIA   I would as eagerly kiss Wookiee lips.
HAN   That can arrangèd be. By heaven's breath,
          A kiss would suit thee well!

                                        [Exit Han Solo.

LEIA   —O man of bile!
          Thou wouldst make e'en the coolest temper burn,
          For thou art made of heat and flame and fire.   90
          No wood may stand within a mile of thee
          But it shall roast as if 'twere on the sun.
          And now, thy scorching manner lights my fuse.
          Aye truly, I confess I am aflame:
          Thine eyes create combustion in my heart,   95
          Thy face doth cause my cheeks to flood with warmth,
          Thy fingers set me trembling at their touch,
          Thy hands may hold the secrets of my soul.
          Thou hast a pow'r o'er Leia's very self,
          Yet wear my patience past what I can bear.   100
          For O, how thou dost needle, jest, and prick
          When thou dost think thy pride is at the stake.
          Be not so full of bile, my noble Han.
          I prithee, choose the tender side of wit.
          If thou couldst ever put thy pride away,   105
          Belike my prejudice would fall aside.
          Then could our two hearts sing a melody,
          Instead of clashing in disharmony.

                                        [Exit Princess Leia.

SCENE 3.

The rebel base on Hoth.

Enter C-3PO *and* R2-D2, *with* HAN SOLO *and*
CHEWBACCA *aside at the* Millennium Falcon.

C-3PO   O R2, thou dost ever plague me so!
E'en now have we been in dishonor sent
Away from our good princess' chamber. Fie!
Such breach of etiquette and protocol,
And all the fault doth on thy shoulders lie.   5

R2-D2   Beep, meep, beep, whistle, meep, beep, squeak,
nee, meep!

C-3PO   Lay not thy blame upon my shoulders, droid—
I did, at no point, ask thee to engage
The thermal heater. 'Twas but a remark
Upon the coldness of the princess' room.   10

R2-D2   Beep, whistle, squeak.

C-3PO   —But freezing it should be!
And now, how shall we dry off all her clothes?
I truly know not how.

R2-D2   —Beep, meep, beep, hoo.

C-3PO   O, switch off!
[C-3PO *walks aside toward the* Millennium Falcon.

R2-D2   [*aside:*]   —Watch thy tongue, thou naughty droid,
Or I shall bring my wit to bear on thee   15
And thou shalt not escape my shocks and jabs.
For though I speak aloud in beeps and squeaks,
Within my mind a keener tongue prevails.
And though thou like a brother art to me,

        I'll happily correct your errant ways.   20
        If thou didst think the thermal heater was
        Too hot, then shalt thou surely not endure
        The fire that I shall kindle with my wit.
                   [C-3PO makes his way to Han Solo.

HAN   *[to Chewbacca:]* Why hast thou taken this apart when
        I am striving to depart this wretched place?   25

C-3PO   Excuse me, Sir.

HAN   —Pray, mend the ship, and swift!

C-3PO   Please, Sir, a word with thee.

HAN   —What dost thou want?

C-3PO   'Tis Princess Leia, Sir, she strives to reach
        Thee on th'communicator.

HAN   —Then 'twas wise
        That I did turn it off, for I have no   30
        Desire to speak with her.

C-3PO   —I see. But she
        Hath after Master Luke made inquiry,
        For surely he hath not return'd unto
        The base. She knows not where he is.

HAN   —In that
        Her mind and mine are one. I know not where   35
        He is.

C-3PO   —But no one knows his whereabouts.

HAN   What dost thou mean by "no one," prating droid?
        Deck officer, deck officer!

               Enter DECK OFFICER.

OFFICER   —Yes, Sir?

HAN   Dost thou know where Commander Skywalker
        Is?

OFFICER   —I've not seen him, but 'tis possible   40
                       He through the entrance to the south return'd.

HAN   "'Tis possible"? I prithee, good lad, go
                       Thou thither and find out. It grows quite dark
                       Outside.

OFFICER   —Aye, Sir.

                                              [Exit deck officer.

C-3PO   —Excuse me, Sir, but may
                       I ask what doth transpire?

HAN   —Thou mayst indeed.   45

C-3PO   O man impossible! Come thou, R2,
                       Let us return unto the princess now.
                       The drying of her clothes is now the least
                       Of all our worries, for another ill
                       Far greater than our mishap is afoot.   50
                       In confidence I tell thee: I do fear
                       That Master Luke grave danger doth confront.

                              [Exit C-3PO and R2-D2.

HAN   What portents strange, what evil tidings this:
                       My friend by no one seen, the droids afraid,
                       Chewbacca prone to error with the ship,   55
                       The young deck officer so tentative—
                       These things foretell some ill that shall occur.
                       But if misfortune toucheth anyone,
                       Let it be me and not my partner, Luke.
                       For he is like a brother unto me,   60
                       As all who fight with me in battle are.
                       Though I did save him in the Death Star clash,
                       'Tis he hath sav'd me from the smuggler's life
                       By leading me on paths more true than I
                       Had e'er foreseen. Now do I call him friend,   65

And this rebellion is the cause we share.
From all my friends here I would not depart
If I were not by Jabba hunted down.
Aye, I would give my bones—my life—for great
Rebellion's sake if e'er it were requir'd.   70
But soft you now: the officer returns.

Enter DECK OFFICER.

OFFICER   Good Sir, Commander Skywalker hath not
Come in the entrance to the south. He may
Have but forgotten to check in.
HAN   —Nay, nay.
His nature is not thus. Now tell me, are   75
The speeders ready?
OFFICER   —Nay, we have not yet
Adapted them unto the cold of Hoth.
HAN   So then upon a tauntaun's back I'll ride.
Though with especial foulness they abuse
My nose, they are the speediest we have.   80
OFFICER   But Sir, the temp'rature doth drop too fast
For any living being to survive.
HAN   'Tis true, and my dear friend doth bear the brunt.
He shall not die while I have life or breath,
For neither snow nor ice nor gloom of Hoth   85
Shall stay my rescue of my greatest friend.
OFFICER   Thy tauntaun shall but freeze ere thou canst ride
Unto our prim'ry marker, I predict.
HAN   Then I shall dine with thee tonight in Hell!
                    [*Exeunt Han Solo, Chewbacca, and deck officer.*

Enter LUKE SKYWALKER, *hanging upside down from balcony.*

LUKE   What warren, friends, is this? I am within 90
      Some icy shelter. Now I do recall—
      The creature large hath ta'en me by surprise,
      Then quickly did my body overpow'r
      By knocking me aside with painful blow.
      It kill'd my tauntaun with its vicious claw, 95
      Unmovèd by the creature's awful scream.
      It must have dragg'd us to this frozen lair.
      E'en now I hear it gnaw my tauntaun's flesh,
      The stench of musty death is in my nose.
      Now I'm awake, hung up by my own feet, 100
      And sounds of tearing skin and crunching bone
      Do echo through the monster's gloomy cave.
      The tauntaun, though, is only the first dish,
      And I am bound to be the second course.
      Indeed, I have a problem grave, and how 105
      Shall I make rescue for myself? But wait—
      What's there—a'lying on the snow nearby?
      It is my lightsaber—how fortunate!
      'Tis still too far to grasp with my own reach:
      Thus call I on the Force to save my life. 110
      O concentrate, and call upon the things
      Thou learn'st from Obi-Wan when he still liv'd.
      Forsooth, I feel the Force begin to flow—
      Within, nearby, inside, surrounding me.
      O Force most strong—the lightsaber's at hand! 115
      Now am I free to flee the fierce beast's clutch,
      But, lo, the creature comes to me anon!
      It will attack me in its fiery rage

Unless I am the first to strike. Lay on!

Enter WAMPA. *Luke cuts off the wampa's arm and exits quickly.*

WAMPA   Alas, how I am by this man abus'd—   120
               Could I, for seeking food, not be excus'd?
               It seemeth that this wampa shall have strife.
               Thus, gentles all: have pity on my life.

                                        [Exit wampa.

SCENE 4.

The rebel base on Hoth.

Enter C-3PO, R2-D2, PRINCESS LEIA, *and* CHEWBACCA.

C-3PO   O horrid interim of waiting, time
               That doth like snail unwillingly creep by.
               Full many hours have pass'd without a word
               Of Master Luke or Captain Solo. Now
               The day grows late, and whisper'd words of fear   5
               Throughout the base are heard for these men's fate.
               It seems that all lose heart, and think the worst,
               For how can e'en our bold Han Solo stand
               The harsh and unrelenting chill of Hoth?
               But now, no more, C-3PO; thou art   10
               Not made to worry and to fret. Be brave!
               Come now, R2, there's no more we can do.
               Behold, my joints are freezing.
R2-D2   —Whistle, hoo.
C-3PO   Say not such things! Of course we shall set eyes
               On Master Luke again. And he shall be   15

In perfect health, thou impish little droid.
Aye, he shall be in perfect health.

R2-D2   [*aside:*]   —I fear
          This chill that doth e'en now my metal frame
          Assault. 'Tis cold unto the core. 'Tis cold,
          I fear, unto the death. Bear up, droid soul,   20
          And listen to C-3PO's advice:
          Be thou a helpful strength amid distress.

          Enter LIEUTENANT *and* MAJOR DERLIN.

LIEUT.   Sir, all patrols are in, and still no sign
          From either Skywalker or Solo.
DERLIN   —Dread!
C-3PO   My Mistress Leia, R2 makes report   25
          He hath not any signals yet receiv'd.
          However, he admitteth that his range
          Is far too weak to give up ev'ry hope.
DERLIN   Your Highness, I do fear there's nothing more
          That we may do tonight. The shield doors must   30
          Be closèd.
LEIA   —I consent, but with a heart
          That breaketh even now.
DERLIN   [*to Lieutenant:*]   —Aye, close the doors.
R2-D2   Meep, beep, meep squeak.
C-3PO   —Now R2 doth report
          The odds of their survival in the cold
          Are seven hundred twenty-five to one.   35
                              [*The shield doors close.*
CHEWBAC. Egh, grrm, egh, auugh!
C-3PO   —Though R2's wont to make

Mistakes, from time to time. O dear, O dear.

[Exeunt Princess Leia, Chewbacca,
Lieutenant, and Major Derlin.

R2-D2   [*aside:*] Why did I speak? O curse my beeping tongue!
"A helpful strength" I pledg'd that I would be,
But now have made these matters worse, for I   40
Have giv'n our princess reason to be scar'd.
Yet I do worry for my master's life,
And though I would not cause undue distress
I fear that he may never make return.
[*To C-3PO:*] Beep, squeak.

C-3PO   —Nay, fear thou not, my silver friend.   45
I'll warrant he shall surely be all right,
For Master Luke is clever, young, and spry
E'en for a human being. So say I!

[Exeunt.

SCENE 5.
The ice world of Hoth.

Enter C-3PO, R2-D2, Princess Leia, *and* Chewbacca.

LUKE   O what a torment have I just endur'd!
For after my attack by creature cruel,
I quickly made my exit from his lair
And made my great escape amidst the snow.
Far, far I ran to find a refuge safe,   5
Yet too far from the rebels' base I've gone.
And now my strength has left—I fail again—
My body falls, too weak to make its way.

[He falls.

Enter GHOST OF OBI-WAN KENOBI.

But now, e'en now, what vision comes to me?

OBI-WAN   Luke!

LUKE   —Ben?

OBI-WAN   —Attend me, Luke. Thou shalt unto   10
            The system Dagobah go.

LUKE   —Dagobah?

OBI-WAN   There thou shalt learn the Force from Yoda, aye—
            The Jedi master who instructed me.

                              [Exit Ghost of Obi-Wan Kenobi.

LUKE   Ben, leave me not! Alas, I fall again.

                              [Luke collapses as Han enters and
                                  dismounts his tauntaun.

HAN   Amid the burning snow and winter's bite,   15
            Have I this journey ta'en to find my friend.
            But lo, what is this sight that now I see?
            'Tis Luke, collaps'd! O lad, be thou not dead!
            Give me some sign thou livest! Aye, Luke, live!
            The cold of Hoth shall yet be warmth to me   20
            If thou art still alive. Come now, good friend!

                              [The tauntaun falls over, frozen to death.

LUKE   [*muttering:*] O Ben, O Dagobah!

                              [Han takes Luke's lightsaber and cuts open
                                  the tauntaun, pulling Luke close to its warmth.

HAN   —We've not much time.
            Stay with me, Luke. 'Tis true, this shall smell bad,
            But also shall it keep thee warm until
            The shelter hath erected been. O, vile!   25
            These tauntauns have an awful stench outside,

But nothing did I know of wretchedness,
Disgusting rot, and sick'ning filth till this
New smell hath made attack upon my nose.

[Han sits with Luke as night passes.

The shelter now is fashion'd by my hands   30
Both strong and deft. We shall await the morn
With only tauntaun's guts as company.
O guardian of nighttime travelers,
Be with me and my comrade Luke this eve,
For we are merely pilgrims far from home   35
Who wish to come again unto our mates.
Now sev'ral anxious hours we've huddl'd here,
And with the morning dawns the light of hope.
My rebel friends shall surely make attempt
To find where Luke and I have spent the night.   40
Search well, my lads, the prize waits to be found!

Enter ZEV *aside, flying.*

ZEV
    The speeders all have been prepar'd, and now
    A proper search for Luke and Han begins.
    But what is this? Shall fortune be so kind?
    My sensors do report some life forms near,   45
    Mayhap the cherish'd find shall yet be mine.
    Pray listen, Echo Base, to my report:
    There's something here my scanner hath just found.
    'Tis yet unsure, but may a life form be.
    Commander Skywalker, dost thou hear me?   50
    'Tis Rogue Two. O good captain Solo, dost
    Thou hear? 'Tis Rogue Two.

HAN
               —Fine good morning, lads,
    'Twas nice of you to fin'lly come around.

ZEV
    Hear, Echo Base: I say, they have been found!

                                 [Exeunt.

SCENE 6.

The rebel base on Hoth.

Enter LUKE SKYWALKER, *reclining on bed.*

LUKE
    Through hazy dreams I have vague memories
    Of being taken to the rebel base
    And given the droid medic's greatest care.
    Now here I am, and naught but scars remain,
    Thus is the creature's foul at last made fair.   5

Enter C-3PO, R2-D2, *and* PRINCESS LEIA.

C-3PO	Good Master Luke, my wires are fill'd with joy
	To see thee fully functional again.
R2-D2	[*aside:*] O that I too could speak aloud!
	[*To Luke:*] Meep, squeak!
C-3PO	R2 expresseth his relief as well!

Enter HAN SOLO *and* CHEWBACCA.

HAN	How goes it with thee, chuck? O verily,	10
	Thou dost look well to me. In faith, thou seem'st	
	E'en strong enough, I'll warr'nt, to pull the ears	
	From off a gundark.	
LUKE	—Truly, thanks to thee.	
HAN	Now thou dost owe me two good turns, my friend.	
	[*To Leia:*] Indeed, Your Worship, well have you	
	conspir'd	15
	To keep me in thy presence longer.	
LEIA	—Fie!	
	'Twas not my doing. Gen'ral Rieekan doth	
	Believe that it is still too dangerous	
	For any ship to leave the system, aye—	
	E'en thy belov'd *Millenn'um Falcon*—till	20
	The shield of energy is active.	
HAN	—Ha!	
	A cloth of fiction thou dost weave, yet I	
	Have found the fatal error in thy stitch:	
	For I believe thou wouldst not let a man	
	So beautiful as I depart from thee.	25
LEIA	The only stitch I know is in my side,	
	From laughing at thy pride most heartily.	
	Thou mayst attempt to needle at my heart,	

But I am sewn of stronger thread than this.
To say I would not let thee go—pish, pish!   30
I know not whence thy great delusions come,
Thou laser brain.
CHEWBAC.   [*laughing:*]   —Gihut, gihut, gihut!
HAN   Aye, laugh indeed, thou fuzzball large. But thou
Hast not seen us alone i' th'passage south,
Where she did unto me unspool, in full,   35
Her feelings true of fondest love for me.
LEIA   My feelings? O! Thou arrogant half-wit,
Thou oversizèd child, thou friend of slime,
Thou man of scruffy looks, thou who herd'st nerfs,
Thou fool-born wimpled roughhewn waste of flesh!   40
HAN   What scruffy? Scruffy, how? Whose scruffiness?
How am I all bescruff'd? [*To Luke:*] Belike my words
Were accurate and hit upon the mark,
Since now she hath her temper lost. True, Luke?
LEIA   Thus is it plain that till thou tam'st thy tongue,   45
No tongue of woman shalt thou comprehend.
                [*Leia kisses Luke at length, then exits.*
CHEWBAC.   Egh, auugh, gihut!
OFFICER   [*from speaker:*]   —All personnel report
Unto the center of command at once.
HAN   [*aside:*] Well hath she play'd the trump.
                [*To Luke:*] Be thou at ease.
             [*Exeunt Han Solo, Chewbacca, C-3PO,*
                        and R2-D2.
LUKE   O kiss most rare, O lips from heaven sent!   50
This is a moment I'll not soon forget.
Though I can sense her heart doth turn to Han,
Still doth this kiss play tricks upon my soul.

By this fair princess I have been bewitch'd—
'Twas ever so since I saw her distress   55
In R2's beam, a'pleading for our help.
But though the lass doth move my heart to joy
I ne'er would tempt her with a word too large,
For shall a Jedi's path lead t'ward romance?
But this sweet kiss I'll hold in mem'ry's vault   60
As a reminder of my noble cause:
To serve rebellion and my princess kind.

                                        [Exit Luke.

Enter HAN SOLO, CHEWBACCA, C-3PO, and R2-D2, crossing to
GENERAL RIEEKAN, the CONTROLLER, and PRINCESS LEIA.

RIEEKAN   A visitor hath come, my princess. 'Tis
            Outside the base, in sector twelve, and doth
            Appear to be directed eastward.
CONTROL.   —'Tis   65
            A thing of metal, cold and harsh and sleek—
            It is not animal.
LEIA   —Well, then 'tis not
            The self-same creature that did harm our Luke.
            But what do ye men think that it may be?
HAN   Belike a speeder, one of ours?
CONTROL.   —Nay, wait.   70
            A signal dim doth reach unto mine ears.
                              [A faint signal is heard.
PROBE   [through comlink:] Beh mena bem bem. Mena bem
                                        bem beh.
C-3PO   Good Sir, six million forms of language do
            I know, and I may tell thee true that this

           Strange signal is not by th'Alliance us'd.   75
           It may, perhaps, be an Imperi'l code.
HAN   'Tis not a friendly sound, that much is sure.
           Now Chewie, come with me and we'll to it.
           [*Aside:*] Snow creatures first, and now Imperi'l droids,
           What portents of great evil may these be?   80
           Though I am brave, forsooth these signs do make
           E'en my courageous heart begin to fear.
           I find myself afraid of what may come,
           That my whole soul shall freeze ere this is done.
           [*To all:*] Chewbacca and myself have ventur'd out   85
           To see the probe. Now Chewie gives a shout—
           It fires on him, and I respond in turn.
           Be gone, thou enemy of all that's right.
           But wait, now what hath happen'd? I releas'd
           A blast most simple—aye, a single blast.   90
           Yet it appears that single blast was all
           It could withstand; the blast was lethal, friends.
           Now naught is left, for it hath been destroy'd.
LEIA   What was't?
HAN   —A droid. My blast did not strike hard,
           Belike the thing did self-destruct.
LEIA   —'Tis clear!   95
           A probe droid from the Empire. This doth mean
           The start of our rebellion's flight from Hoth,
           For now that we discoverèd have been
           We lack security.
HAN   —Agreed. Methinks
           The Empire knoweth we are here on Hoth.   100
           [*Aside:*] My sense of doom and dread is not without
           Its cause, for this event is grave indeed.

RIEEKAN   Good friends, dear rebels, comrades one and all,
           We have no choice but to flee hastily.
           Our swift evacuation shall commence,   105
           And till 'tis done, make ready our defense.

                                          [*Exeunt.*

SCENE 7.

Aboard the Empire's Super Star Destroyer.

Enter ADMIRAL OZZEL, GENERAL VEERS,
and CAPTAIN PIETT.

PIETT   My admiral?
OZZEL   —Yes, Captain.
PIETT   —Here's a thing
           That thou shouldst see, good Sir. We have receiv'd
           Report from a Hoth system probe, the best
           That we have found so far.
OZZEL   —Your best, belike,
           Shall bested be, for thousands of these probes   5
           We have a'wandering the galaxy
           And looking for the rebels. I want proof,
           Piett, not leads. Proof—only that—is best.
PIETT   But Sir, this best is better yet, for it
           Hath found some forms of life upon the ground.   10
OZZEL   How better yet? How best? It could be but
           An error or some useless reading. If
           We were to follow ev'ry lead, our best
           Would soon turn worst.
PIETT   —And yet I do maintain

My best is better yet for this: 'tis said   15
That Hoth is all devoid of human forms.
It seems, good Sir, the rebels have been found.
Why else would sign of life appear on Hoth?
I'll warrant, Sir, my forecast shall prevail.

Enter DARTH VADER.

VADER   You have found something good?
PIETT   —My Lord, we have.   20
            A probe that late hath made descent on Hoth
            Hath made discovery of both life forms
            And the appearance of a power source.
                            [Piett shows Vader the screen.
VADER   Thy judgment hath prov'd best, Piett: 'tis them.
            Forsooth, the rebels may be found therein.   25
OZZEL   My Lord, there are throughout the galaxy
            So many settlements we have not mapp'd.
            This could be smugglers, maybe even—
VADER   —Nay,
            That is the system, certain am I of't,
            And Skywalker is with them there. Now set   30
            Thy course t'ward Hoth, and Gen'ral Veers, prepare
            Your men for combat.
                    [Exeunt Admiral Ozzel, General Veers,
                                and Captain Piett.
                —Hath not a Sith eyes?
            Hath not a Sith such feelings, heart, and soul,
            As any Jedi Knight did e'er possess?
            If you prick us, do we not bleed? If you   35
            Blast us, shall we not injur'd be? If you

Assault with lightsaber, do we not die?
I have a body as do other men,
Though made, in part, of wires and steel. And aye,
I vari'us passions feel, as all men do.   40
So I, a Sith, shall not distracted be
Till I attain the thing for which I seek.
Therefore I shall pursue this Skywalker
Unto the limit of the galaxy.
For true, he hath the Death Star quite destroy'd,   45
And true, he hath the Force with him as well.
But truly, more than that the boy doth have—
For truth be told, his name doth stir my soul.
The boy's connection to myself I do
Not understand as yet. This Skywalker   50
Must have some link to my life past, but what?
So shall this Sith pursue this rebel lad,
And find the missing truth of Vader's life.

Enter GENERAL VEERS.

VADER   What news dost thou have, Gen'ral Veers?
VEERS   —My Lord,
         Our noble fleet hath flown to Hoth in haste   55
         With hopes to catch the rebels by surprise.
         The fleet has movèd out of lightspeed now,
         But com-scan hath detected a sharp shield
         Of energy surrounding planet six
         Within the system. It is strong enough   60
         To hinder what bombardment we can make.
         This grim news I report with sadden'd mien:
         It seems, my Lord, our fleet is all too close.

VADER	The rebels are aware of our attack,
	For Adm'ral Ozzel left lightspeed too near 65
	To the Hoth system.
VEERS	—He believ'd surprise
	Was wiser . . .
VADER	—Say no more. Speak not to his
	Defense. He is as clumsy as he is
	Replete with ignorance. Prepare your troops
	Now, Veers, to lead a ground attack. We shall 70
	Still win the day, despite the blunder.
VEERS	—Aye.

[Exit General Veers.

VADER *hails* ADMIRAL OZZEL *and* CAPTAIN PIETT,
who enter by balcony.

OZZEL	Lord Vader, I am happy to report
	The fleet has come out of lightspeed and is
	Prepar'd to—

[*Darth Vader begins to choke Admiral Ozzel
using the Force.*

VADER	—Thou hast fail'd me once again,
	But nevermore shalt thou have chance to fail. 75
	I bring the Force to bear upon thy throat
	That thou, in thy last breath, shalt know my pow'r.
	Captain Piett?
PIETT	—My Lord?
VADER	—Prepare to land
	Our troops beyond the shield of energy,
	And then deploy our fleet so naught can 'scape 80
	The system. Do it, Admiral Piett.

And be thou sure to rise to thy new rank.

          [Admiral Ozzel dies. Exit Darth Vader.

PIETT   Alas, with this promotion comes some dread,

           For Vader hath no rev'rence for the head.

                             [Exit.

ACT II

SCENE 1.

The rebel base on Hoth.

Enter HAN SOLO *and* CHEWBACCA,
working on the Millennium Falcon
with a MAINTENANCE DROID.

HAN   A pilot must respect his ship with care,
And play physician to her ev'ry need.
With patience and with tender healing touch
I caringly embrace each bolt and wire.
Now, 'tis repair'd. [*To Chewbacca:*] Good Chewie,
                         try it now!   5

CHEWBAC.   Egh.
                   [*The ship begins to smoke and spark.*

HAN   —Nay! Act thou with speed, and turn it off!
[*Aside:*] Physician, heal thyself from too much haste.

Enter LUKE SKYWALKER.

LUKE   [*aside:*] The last time I said my farewell to these
Compatriots of mine, 'twas ere the Death
Star battle when it seem'd as though they were   10
Deserting us. But now, their valor prov'd,
Their hearts align'd with good Rebellion's cause,
I'll wish them on their merry way with joy.
[*To Chewbacca:*] Chewbacca, brave, 'tis now my time
                            to leave,
For soon to Dagobah my path is bound.   15

CHEWBAC.   [*embracing Luke:*] Egh!

LUKE   —How your tight embrace doth warm my heart—
                  But also strains my bones, thou jolly brute.
HAN   Well met, young lad. [*To droid:*] There must a reason be
                  Why this malfunction hath occur'd. But now,
                  I prithee, get thee hence.
                                                    [*Exit maintenance droid.*
                                    Art thou yet well?   20
LUKE   Aye, verily. [*Aside:*] O what words would I say
                  To this man here, if words were loud enough!
                  But hath a word e'er been created, which
                  Could tell the comrade's love I feel for him,
                  Articulate the good I sense in him,   25
                  Express the debt of life I owe to him?
                  At times 'tis true that words betray us all—
                  The mighty pow'r of language fails to speak,
                  And neither tongue nor rhetoric gives aid.
                  This Han hath found a life among our band   30
                  That did transform his former, solo self,
                  But now he takes his leave to pay the price
                  Of former indiscretions come to call.
                  I would explain how much he means to me,
                  I would disclose my deep respect for him,   35
                  I would unveil my brotherlike regard,
                  I would reveal the workings of my soul—
                  But at this moment words are render'd weak.
                  Thus, he must see the story in my eyes,
                  Peruse the tale that's told within my heart,   40
                  And there read more than ever can be penn'd.
HAN   Now be thou careful, friend.
LUKE   —And thou as well.
                                                    [*Exit Luke Skywalker.*

HAN   A noble lad, and true. If Fate is kind,
             I shall make right the danger I am in
             And live to fight aside him once again.   45

                    [Exeunt Han Solo and Chewbacca.

         Enter the CONTROLLER *and* GENERAL RIEEKAN.

CONTROL.   My general, a group of Star Destroy'rs
             Has just emerg'd from hyperspace, and now
             Has been detected in yon sector four.
RIEEKAN   Divert all pow'r unto our forward shield.
             In doing so we may protect the base   50
             Until the transports their escape have made.
             Then, let us all prepare for ground assault.
             [*To all:*] Good gentlemen and women, come ye near!
             For we shall now our very lives defend.

             Enter REBEL PILOTS, *including* HOBBIE *and*
                 MAJOR DERLIN, *and* PRINCESS LEIA.

LEIA   Good cheer! All preparation hath been made,   55
             Both for the swift retreat of transports hence,
             And to defend our base until they're fled.
             The carriers shall meet up at the north,
             And larger transports leave once they are full.
             Two fighter escorts shall be sent with each   60
             And shall remain quite close, for our strong shield
             Will be disarm'd a fleeting length of time.
             'Twill be a passage dangerous no doubt,
             But with the Force we shall prevail, indeed.
HOBBIE   I prithee, say again: shall only two   65

	Of our small fighters match a Star Destroy'r?
LEIA	Pray, screw your courage to the sticking place.

LEIA   Of our small fighters match a Star Destroy'r?
Pray, screw your courage to the sticking place.
Our ion cannons shall with lethal fire
Make ev'ry pathway clear. When you have clear'd
The shield of energy, then go anon   70
Unto our rendezvous. Do all agree?
Will ye all go in great rebellion's name?

ALL   Aye, Princess, aye!

HOBBIE   —We shall heed thy command.

DERLIN   Now ev'ryone unto their stations, go!

    [Exeunt rebel pilots, including Hobbie
    and Lieutenant Derlin.

RIEEKAN   *[to Controller:]* Belike the power generators will   75
Their prim'ry target be. Prepare thou now
To open up the shield. And may the Force
Attend our swift retreat, our hearts inspire!

CONTROL.   Now standby ion cannon; aye, and fire.

    [Exeunt.

S C E N E   2 .
The ice world of Hoth.

Enter CHORUS.

CHORUS   The transports make their way deep into space;
The ion cannon leads as they take flight.
But now the rebels grave new dangers face,
As th'Empire sends a ground assault to fight.

Enter LUKE SKYWALKER *and* DACK, *his copilot, with* REBEL PILOTS,
including WEDGE ANTILLES, JANSON, *and* ZEV.

DACK   How dost thou fare, good Sir? For I have heard   5
              Of your unlucky recent incident.
              How is it with thee after the attack?
LUKE   Quite well, I thank thee, Dack. And art thou well?
DACK   Aye, truthfully, Commander—I do feel
              I could the Empire overthrow myself,   10
              If I were giv'n the opportunity.
              A single warrior to bring them down,
              A single hand to show rebellion's strength,
              A single mind that could outwit them all,
              A single Dack to best the Empire's might.   15
LUKE   O noble soul, how like a soldier said!
              It seems that thou and I are fashion'd from
              One cloth—one fabric knits our souls together.
              The feeling you express is one I've known.
              Indeed, it is a potent privilege,   20
              But also brings responsibility.

Enter AT-ATs 1, 2, *and* 3, *giant Imperial walkers, on other side.*

AT-AT 1   But who did bid thee join with us?
AT-AT 3   —Piett.
                 'Twas he who order'd me to come with ye
                 To crush the rebels and their little base.
AT-AT 2   Well said, for I know of no baser base—   25
                 'Twill be a vict'ry great when 'tis destroy'd.
                 But think ye we shall in this fight prevail?
                 The rebels are a force formidable.

AT-AT 1   My friends, we have had quite enough of talk:

The battle is upon us, let us go.   30

And ye who doubt, I pray remember this:

Although we are but AT-ATs gray and plain,

We have a noble task to undertake—

Our mighty Emperor's reign to protect,

The great Darth Vader to obey and aid,   35

And Admiral Piett to serve with pride.

So shall an AT-AT swoon before the fight,

Or should our legs be shaken ere th'assault?

Have we been made to cower? I say nay!

An AT-AT should be made of sterner stuff.   40

AT-AT 3   [*to AT-AT 2:*] I pray, good walker, is he ever thus?

AT-AT 2   Aye, truly, Sir, I never yet have met

An All Terrain Armorèd Transport who

Is loftier of mind than this one here.

Indeed, although like us he's made of steel,   45

He never enters battle zones unless

He hath made some great speech to steel his nerves.
It does no harm.

AT-AT 3   —No harm, but to mine ears.
I'd rather fight than hear another speech.

AT-AT 1   Now let us go, these rebels to destroy!   50
> [The AT-ATs advance on Luke Skywalker
> and other rebel pilots.

LUKE   [to rebel pilots:] Now stay together, men.

DACK   —Alas, good Luke,
The ship's computer hath malfunction'd. O,
I am not set for this attack!

LUKE   —Be patient.
We shall use pattern delta now, anon!
> [Rebels and AT-ATs duel, and
> rebels quickly retreat.

A hit! A very palpable hit. Wait,   55
Although my shots have found their mark, their blasts
Have no effect. It is their armor, fie!
Our blasters are too weak to penetrate
The strength of their robust exteriors.
Rogue group, use thy harpoons and cables, too.   60
Let us go for their legs and trip them up—
Perhaps they may be bested from beneath.
Dack, art thou with me?

DACK   —This malfunction hath
Put fire into the system. I'll attempt
To quickly gain some pow'r another way.   65

LUKE   I prithee, be thou careful now, young Dack!
> [The fight resumes. Dack is struck.

DACK   Alas, I die! Farewell, Commander Luke!
> [Dack dies.

LUKE   Nay, Dack! O agony of battle, curse
            Of war, and dread of ev'ry soldier's heart:
            To suffer at the hands of enemies,   70
            To end one's days by pow'r of the unjust!
            What use is war? For it doth ravage all
            Within its path, and what hath it e'er solv'd?
            'Tis rare that peace doth follow in war's wake.
            Indeed, this recent blow doth only urge   75
            And heighten my destructive sentiments:
            I shall avenge thee, Dack, and slay these here
            Who have thy lifeblood ta'en, and seal'd thy fate.

AT-AT 2   No more of these amusements with the weak.
            'Tis time to make this victory our own: 80
            Head for the power generator, mates,
            The battle's nearly won!

LUKE   —Rogue Three, dost hear?

WEDGE   I do, Rogue Leader.

LUKE   —Wedge, I need thee now.
            I've lost my gunner: thou must strike their legs
            With thy harpoon. I'll give thee aid—we'll fly   85
            Together, follow close behind me.

WEDGE   —Aye!
            Now activate harpoon and slay these beasts!

            [The fight resumes. Wedge and his gunner, Janson,
                    strike AT-AT 1 with a rope around the legs.

AT-AT 1   What treachery! The rebels have assail'd
            My weakest part. My legs, good comrades—they
            Have struck where I most vulnerable am.   90

WEDGE   Well hit, brave Janson. Now encircle him
            And bring this giant down to meet his end.
            It worketh, friends! His legs hath been confin'd,

And thus the brute hath trouble with his stride.

Just one more pass around, and then detach!   95

JANSON   The cable is detach'd! He falls!

AT-AT 1   —Alack;

I perish now, my comrades. Win the day!

[AT-AT 1 falls and dies.

WEDGE   A-ha!—and thus our Dack hath been aveng'd!

LUKE   I see thy handiwork; well done, strong Wedge.

Dack's memory we honor by this strike.   100

AT-AT 2   The rebels have destroy'd one of our lot,

But we shall yet o'erwhelm them utterly.

I'll make approach unto their hidden base,

Identify their systems in my sights,

And then shall on the generator fire.   105

LUKE   Rogue Two, art thou beside me in this fight?

We need the help of ev'ry fighter here.

Not long ago thou rescu'd Han and me

From our meek shelter on the ice of Hoth:

Thou art a man of cunning, strength, and wit.   110

And thus I ask thee on thy honor, Sir:

Art thou prepar'd to face this harsh assault?

ZEV   Aye, verily, Rogue Leader, that I am.

My life I am prepar'd to sacrifice

To save rebellion from this fierce attack.   115

LUKE   Then let us all approach the knaves again.

Prepare your swift harpoon and we shall strike!

AT-AT 3   They think themselves the noble ones, but we

Defend the Emp'ror's righteousness today.

AT-AT 2   Well spoken. Let us fight for Empire's might!   120

[They duel again.

ZEV   O Luke, I have been hit, and die anon!

Remember me whene'er thou speak'st of this.
        [Zev is slain. Luke is struck and falls to the ground.

LUKE   Alas, poor Zev. Too many lost—such good
        And worthy men have met their end to these
        Confounded walkers. Fie! This battle bleak   125
        May mean Rebellion's end. 'Tis now my turn—
        My ship hath ta'en a hit. I fall, yet am
        Not slain. Indeed, though here I lie upon
        The ground, I spy an opportunity.
        For while this awful monster walks above,   130
        I spy his weakness as I lie below.
        He passes just beyond me—now to it!
        Revenge should have no bounds when friends are
                                        slain,
        And now their memory doth push me on.
        My lightsaber shall strike the lethal blow;   135
        I'll hit where he shall feel it, in his heart—
        If ever such cruel beast did have a heart.
                [Luke strikes AT-AT 3 from below,
                        and AT-AT 3 dies.

AT-AT 3   I perish, comrade true, but fall with pride!
AT-AT 2   Although my fellow AT-ATs meet their ends,
        I press toward my goal with purpose firm.   140
        The rebels' power generator is
        Within the target of my lasers keen.
        Now all the fallen AT-ATs I salute
        As for my noble Emperor I shoot!
                [He shoots and destroys the power generator.
                        Exeunt all, in confusion.

SCENE 3.

The rebel base on Hoth.

Enter GENERAL RIEEKAN *and*
PRINCESS LEIA, *with an aide.*

RIEEKAN   Our pow'r is insufficient to protect
            Two transports at one time.
LEIA   —'Tis risky, aye,
            But this base overpower'd is, and shall,
            I fear, withstand no more of this attack.
            We have no choice.
RIEEKAN   —Indeed, thou speakest true.   5
            [*Into comlink:*] Launch all patrols.
LEIA   [*to aide:*]   —Evacuate the staff
            Who do remain within the base. Make haste!

Enter HAN SOLO *and* CHEWBACCA *on balcony,*
repairing the Millennium Falcon.

HAN   These endless fixes now are nearly done,
            And soon we may take flight. 'Tis none too soon—
            This base shall not survive this great attack.   10
CHEWBAC.   Auugh!
HAN   —Nay, nay! This one here and that one there.
            'Tis clear? [*Aside:*] I do admit this Wookiee here is dear,
            But if he break my ship I'll break his pate!

Enter C-3PO *with* R2-D2, *aside.*

C-3PO   My R2 small, pray be thou safe, good friend,

And take especial care of Master Luke.   15
Farewell, farewell! Parting is such sweet sorrow
That I shall say farewell till thou hast left.

R2-D2   [*aside:*] "Till thou hast left"? No poet he, indeed.
Alas, it seems that romance is not one
Of 3PO's six million forms of speech.   20

     [Exit R2-D2. C-3PO moves to Princess Leia and
     General Rieekan. Loud sounds of shaking are heard.

HAN   O zounds! What is this pow'rful shaking here?
The base begins to crumble even now.
Our humble shelter made of snow and ice
Is now defeated by the Empire's might
And starts to fall apart. O, shall we too?   25
Shall our rebellion suffer this same Fate—
To be destroyèd by the Empire cruel?
To be demolish'd by Imperi'l strength?
Though I had plann'd to go and save myself
From Jabba's bounty hunters, I cannot: 30
This smuggler-captain never shall desert
Whilst friends nearby do mortal peril face.
I shall not steal away and leave behind
The princess who doth lead the rebels true.
She is of great importance, and my life   35
Must be but secondary to her fate.
So shall I take her in the *Falcon* swift
And spirit her away to someplace safe.
'Tis not because of how I feel about
Her, nay; naught there of love, that much is true—   40
Or if 'tis not, I'll tell myself it is.
Now to it, Han, ere our great cause is lost.

     [Han Solo moves to General Rieekan
     and Princess Leia.

	Your Worship, art thou well?
LEIA	—O, wherefore art
	Thou yet within this base? Hast thou not fled?
HAN	The center of command has been struck down. 45
LEIA	And yet hast thou thy clearance to depart.
HAN	Depart I shall, but first deliver thee
	Unto thy ship.
C-3PO	—Your Highness, we must take
	This final transport. 'Tis our only hope!

[A blast is heard, closer.

OFFICER	[*through comlink:*] Imperi'l troops have come into
	the base! 50
	Imperi'l troops have come into the base!
HAN	Now end thy stubborn ways, and set aside
	Thy prejudice. Thou wilt come with me now,
	I do command it. Neither argument
	Nor moving speech nor aught that thou canst say 55
	Shall sway me now: thou wilt come with me, Princess.
LEIA	[*aside:*] O noble man, protector of my soul!
	[*To aide:*] Send our evacuation code and get
	Thee to thy transport.

[Exeunt General Rieekan and aide. Han Solo and
Princess Leia begin to walk toward the transport.

| C-3PO | —Prithee, wait for me! |

[As they make their way to the ship,
a wall falls in their path.

HAN	The battle is within the very walls, 60
	And ev'ry portent tells of dread and doom.
	[*Into comlink:*] Good transport, this is Solo. Take
	your leave—
	Our way has now become a wayward thing,

All fill'd with mounds of ice that block our path.
This moment calls for quick decision. Thus,   65
I shall with Leia flee on *Falcon*'s wings.
> [*Han Solo and Princess Leia run the other way,*
> *toward the* Millennium Falcon, *shutting*
> *the door against C-3PO.*

C-3PO But wait, where do you go? Pray, do come back!
Most typical this is. O wretched fate,
To be deserted by my friends most dear.
These human beings care but little for   70
Us droids who ever serve with loyalty.
Thus shall I end my days within this base,
A frozen remnant of the rebels' stay
On Hoth. Belike one day explorers shall
Discover this defeated base, shall dig   75
Into its core and find a golden droid
Whose final resting place was ice and snow.
"Who would abandon such a lovely droid?"
No doubt this shall be their response when they
Espy me here. "What wretched humans would   80
Leave such a one as this alone to rot?"
I shudder at this thought, let it not be!
O open up your hearts unto my kind,
Then open wide this door for kindness' sake!
> [*The door opens.*

HAN   Anon, thou goldenrod, thou heap of scrap,   85
Else shalt thou ever stay within this base
And make thyself a lasting icy grave.

C-3PO [*aside:*] This man is both the reason for my pain
And for my joy. My gratitude o'erflows!
> [*They enter the* Millennium Falcon.

HAN   [*to Chewbacca:*] Now wherefore doth the ship not
                                                    function right?   90
LEIA   Pray, would it help if I did disembark
              And push with all a princess' might upon't?
HAN   Belike!
C-3PO   —Pray, Captain Solo, Captain Solo!
HAN   Tut!
C-3PO   —It shall wait.
LEIA   —This bucket full of bolts
              Shall ne'er beyond that blockade make escape.   95
              We may as well depart the base aboard
              A tauntaun's furry back!
HAN   —The ship hath yet
              Surprising, keen maneuvers, sweetheart. Watch!
              The ship protects us with its lasers true
              Against th'Imperi'l troops who come at us.   100
              See, Princess, see? Now Chewie, let us fly,
              And hope we shall not burn the engine out.
              Repairs are made—let us repair to space!
LEIA   One day thou shalt be wrong, and well I hope
              I shall bear witness to thy failure great.   105
HAN   Anon, Chewbacca, lead us to our fate!
                        [*Exeunt in the* Millennium Falcon.

SCENE 4.
The rebel base on Hoth.

Enter LUKE SKYWALKER *and* R2-D2.

LUKE   The recent battle is both lost and won:

'Tis lost because of rebels who expir'd,
'Tis lost because our base is compromis'd,
'Tis lost because our time on Hoth is done,
'Tis lost because we now evacuate.   5
And yet, 'tis won because two walkers fell,
'Tis won because the foes arriv'd too late,
'Tis won because our transport is away,
'Tis won because we live to fight again.
R2, we leave anon. With all due speed   10
Prepare the ship for takeoff.

R2-D2   —Meep, beep, squeak!

LUKE   Fear not, R2, for now we fly!

R2-D2   —Beep, hoo.

LUKE   Now flies my weary soul to Dagobah,
The place that hath in vision called to me.
I know not what or who this Yoda is,   15
Yet do I trust the ghost of my dear Ben.
To be a Jedi is my calling now,
To learn the ways of the most potent Force.
Already have I had more mentors than
Most people would e'er know in seven lives.   20
But here I am, drawn t'ward another quest—
To travel to an unknown system, aye,
And meet an unknown person who, perhaps,
Doth not expect my sudden visit there.
Yet I believe the words that came from Ben   25
Were better than a foolproof prophet's tale.
There is a tide in the affairs of Jedi,
Which taken at the flood, leads to the Force.
Omitted, all the voyage of their life
Is bound in black holes and in miseries.   30

On such a full sea I am now afloat.
And I must take the current where it serves,
Or lose my chance to find my destiny.

R2-D2 [*aside:*] O noble speech, with feeling brute and raw.
My master's honor shall I serve with pride.   35
How best to show him I stand by his side?
I'll offer ways to help him navigate.
[*To Luke:*] Beep, meep, meep, squeak, beep, whistle,
                                   whistle, beep?

LUKE Nay, nothing's wrong, I merely change our course.

R2-D2 Meep, beep, squeak, whistle, beep, meep, meep,
                                     beep, whee?   40

LUKE We shall not rendezvous with our friends yet.
Unto the system Dagobah we travel—
And what we shall meet there, time shall unravel.

                                        [*Exeunt.*

SCENE 5.

Space, in the cockpit of the Millennium Falcon.

Enter HAN SOLO, CHEWBACCA, *and* PRINCESS LEIA.

HAN Hoth is a memory, but trouble still
Doth follow close behind. With threat'ning force
The Empire's ships aggressively pursue
My well-belovèd ship. Shall we escape?

CHEWBAC. Auugh!

HAN   —Truly, Chewie, I did see them too!   5

LEIA I prithee, say—what hast thou seen, O Han?

HAN Two Star Destroyers coming t'ward the ship.

Enter C-3PO.

C-3PO	Sir, Sir, may I but say a thing to thee?
HAN	Pray, shut him up or shut him down, anon!
	Prepare our shield—they still may be outrun. 10
	[*Aside:*] With all my pilot's wisdom, skill, and might
	I shall attempt to outwit these who chase.
	Now watch, you Empire vile, how I do fly!
	First up and down, aye, up and down, this Han
	Will lead them up and down. Away we go! 15
	Now back and forth, then back around again.
	They are confounded by my errant moves.
	Ha, ha! They are confus'd and fall behind.
	Thus we have slipp'd away, soon safe from harm.
	[*To Chewbacca:*] Make ready for the jump to
	hyperspace. 20
C-3PO	But Sir!
LEIA	—They do approach!
HAN	—Not yet: observe!
	[*The* Millennium Falcon *makes a sound and fails.*
LEIA	Observe? What's to observe, pray tell me plain?
HAN	A fig! The ship seems to malfunction. Fie!
	'Tis possible we may in trouble be.
C-3PO	I tried to warn thee, Sir, the hyperdrive 25
	Hath damag'd been, and cannot do its task!
	Lightspeed is verily unfeasible!
HAN	Correction: we in trouble truly are.
	O that all I had fix'd were truly fix'd!
	But now I must in haste—and under threat 30
	Of death—attempt to fix the ship once more.
	[*He runs to repair the ship, yelling back*
	to Chewbacca.

	Where are the horizontal boosters hid?
CHEWBAC.	Egh, auugh!
HAN	—Alluvi'l dampers, where are they?

[*Aside:*] If only I were but more organiz'd!

'Tis true that order's not a smuggler's gift.   35

[*To Chewbacca:*] Bring me the hydrospanners quickly
                                       now.

[*Aside:*] I know not how we shall escape this time.

Of all the situations I have seen,

Of all the problems small or dangers great,

Of all the rubs and scrapes have scratch'd my life,   40

Of all the enemies just barely fled—

This moment now doth seem the worst of all.
                 [*Loud sound. Han is knocked aside.*

Alack, now what is this? What shakes the ship?

How have we gone from bad to still worse yet?

LEIA	Good Han, return at once!

                 [*Han runs back to the cockpit.*

                   'Tis asteroids!   45

HAN	[*aside:*] O wicked thought and wonderful idea

That cometh to me in this frightful time.

I shall here chart a course none would expect:

Not flee from danger, nay, but welcome it,

And in so doing break the Empire's grip   50

While rescuing my princess from all harm.

[*To Chewbacca:*] Set course two-seven-one.

LEIA	—What didst thou say?

Thou wilt not enter in the ast'roid field?

For certain thou art wild—but not insane!

HAN	Yet they would be the madder to give chase. 55
LEIA	Thou must not do this to impress me, Han.

[*Aside:*] Already he hath won my heart, 'tis true,
Yet would I rather live to tell him so!

C-3PO   Good Sir, attend: the possibility
Of navigating fields of ast'roids is   60
Three thousand seven hundred twenty to
But one—the odds are well against thee here!

HAN   The odds of rescuing a princess: low.
The odds of smuggler turning rebel: lower.
The odds of ending th'Death Star: lowest yet!   65
I tell thee, droid: assail me not with odds!

LEIA   [*aside:*] Behold, what keen maneuvers doth he make,
And how, like Gungans sinking in the swamp,
Our enemies do fall behind us, slain.
What bravery he showeth for my sake.   70

HAN   If you recall, Your Highness, you did hope
You would bear witness to my failure great:
It may be now.

LEIA   —My word I do rescind.
We shall be pulveriz'd if we remain
A'floating in this field of wayward rocks.   75
Thou hast thy honor proven, Han, now please:
Let us seek safety in another place.

HAN   I cannot argue with thine argument.
I shall attempt to fly us closer in
Toward a larger ast'roid.

C-3PO   —Closer?

CHEWBAC.   —Auugh!   80

C-3PO   O this is suicide, for where have we
To go where we may yet survive? Are we
Not bound for death?

HAN   —Aye, this one here shall do.

It hath a goodly look.

LEIA   —What "goodly look"?

HAN   Be calm, I prithee, for it shall suffice.   85

C-3PO   Excuse me, Princess, but where are we bound?

[*The* Millennium Falcon *flies deep*
into one of the asteroids.

LEIA   My hope flies unto you, most worthy man,
My hope for us, and for our safety, too.
I hope it is the Force that leadeth thee,
I hope that thou dost know what thou dost do.   90

HAN   Thy hopes do echo mine, my lady, true.

[*Exeunt into an asteroid's tunnel.*

SCENE 6.

Aboard the Empire's Super Star Destroyer.

Enter ADMIRAL PIETT *with* DARTH VADER, *replacing his mask.*

PIETT   [*aside:*] O sight most tragic, this—a robot-man
Who doth require a mask to stay alive.
What situation e'er did lead to this?
How can he stand to live beneath a mask?
But soft, Piett, and reconsider this: 5
Aye, verily, how shall I judge? The mask
He wears is far more obvious than most.
With Vader it is plain he wears a mask,
Though few have seen the scarring underneath.
But truly, what man doth not wear a mask?   10
For all of us are maskèd in some way—
Some choose sharp cruelty as their outward face,

Some put themselves behind a king's façade,
Some hide behind the mask of bravery,
Some put on the disguise of arrogance.   15
But underneath our masks, are we not one?
Do not all wish for love, and joy, and peace?
And whether rebel or Imperial,
Do not our hearts all beat in time to make
The pounding rhythm of the galaxy?   20
So while Darth Vader's mask keeps him alive,
And sits upon his face for all to see,

'Tis possible he is more honest than
A man who wears no mask, but hides his self.
But come, Piett, now still thy prating tongue—   25
His private time is done, his mask back on.

VADER   Yes, Admiral?

PIETT   —Our ships have found the swift
Millenn'um Falcon, Lord. However, it
Hath ventur'd deep into an ast'roid field.
It seems unsafe to make pursuit therein: 30
To follow it is far too great a risk.

VADER   Thy fear of asteroids concerns me not.
I want the ship, not thy most weak dismay.

PIETT   I understand, my Lord, and shall obey.

                                        [Exeunt.

SCENE 7.

The Dagobah system.

Enter LUKE SKYWALKER *and* R2-D2.

LUKE   What misadventure I have seen today!
Our sensors spied no cities or machines
Within this system desolate, but life
Forms plenty. As we made our way unto
The planet's atmosphere, all went awry: 5
My X-wing ship began to shake and groan.
My scopes had fail'd, and I did blindly spin
Into a landing doom'd to end with strife.
'Tis almost fortunate that I did land
Within this swampy bog where now the ship   10

Is partway sunk, for had I hit the ground
My ship and droid and even my own self
Might have been crush'd, and ev'rything destroy'd.
But now my ship is fixèd in the mire,
And how it shall come out I cannot tell.   15
Was this first trouble all I would endure?
Nay, nay! It seemeth Fate did not see fit
To send pain singular, but multiple!
Fate hath provided pains abundantly,
For this is not the end of our distress.   20
As R2 and I headed for the shore
He fell into the water, wheels to scope,
And was assaulted by a mighty beast—
Aye, swallow'd whole and disappear'd from sight.
For seeming ages I did search for him,   25
To no avail. And then, with frightful scream,
He was ejected from the swamp as fast
As proton-fill'd torpedoes from their shaft.
Above my head he sail'd, well o'er the ground,
And landed in a heap of dirt and grime.   30
'Twas only for his metal-tasting shell
This little droid shall live to see tomorrow.
So much misfortune! After all this pain
I should feel grateful still to have my life.
But now we are maroon'd within a place   35
Where neither friend nor contact may be found.
I should have listen'd to the wise R2
When he said coming here would work us woe.
Our camp is now set up, our food prepar'd,
My faithful R2 chargeth up his pow'r,   40
The semblance of good order we present—

But I have neither stomach nor desire
To sit down to a hale and hearty feast.
More pressing, too, I must this Yoda find,
Indeed, if that good man doth e'en exist.   45
Look 'round about, R2: is this place not
Unlikely for a Jedi master's home?
'Tis strange, 'tis passing strange, 'tis pitiful.

R2-D2   Beep, squeak?

Enter YODA, *hidden behind.*

LUKE   —I know not what it is, dear friend.
'Tis like some thing appearing from a dream,   50
Some midnight reverie I cannot shake.
For neither does this circumstance seem real,
Nor do I slumber here—aye, that I know.
It seems the place is but a walking shadow—
Not dream, not wake, but something in between.   55
The strangeness of the scene creeps in my bones,
Yet also do I feel familiar pangs.

R2-D2   Beep, whistle, meep?

LUKE   —I know not. I do feel—
                        [Yoda reveals himself.

YODA   What dost thou feel, hmm?
Prithee, I would truly know   60
What is it thou feel'st?
                        [Luke points his blaster at Yoda.

LUKE   That odd, familiar sense that we are watch'd!

R2-D2   Beep, beep, meep, whistle, beep, squeak, whistle, nee!

YODA   Away with weapons!
I mean no harm, but wonder   65

Why thou hast come here.

LUKE   Thou sneaking imp! I look for someone here.

YODA   Looking, are you, hmm?
Found someone you have, it seems!
Is that not correct?   70

LUKE   'Tis true, I may suppose—I've someone found,
Though such a one as this did not expect.

YODA   Help you I can, aye.
[*Aside:*] I, indeed, more help shall be
Than he imagines.   75

LUKE   Nay, I think not. My search is for a great
And mighty warrior, a man of strength!

YODA   O, great warrior!
A great warrior you seek?
Wars not make one great.   80

But soft, no more of
Talking, for my appetite
Dinner demandeth.

Thus shall I explore
The food thou hast here prepar'd.   85
Mmm, and I shall taste.

LUKE   Nay, nay, unhand my supper, little one!

YODA   How dost grow so big
When the food of thy diet
Is of this strange kind?   90

LUKE   Attend, my friend, thou must leave this alone.
My food I shall have need of, as we strive
To free our ship. I did not try to land
Inside that puddle drear, and if we could

Our ship remove, we would. But we cannot—   95
At least, I know not how it shall be done.
    [Yoda rummages through Luke's supplies,
      discarding them to the ground.

YODA Unfortunate ship . . .
Thou canst not get it out, hmm?
O, what merry light!
    [Yoda removes a light from Luke's supplies.

LUKE A mess thou now hast made! Give me that light!   100
YODA 'Tis mine, it is mine!
I shall the pretty thing have
Or I help you not.
LUKE I need not thine assistance, nay! I need
My lamp, for it shall guide me out of this   105
Most slimy and disgusting hole of mud!
YODA What slimy, what mud?
Thou speak'st indeed of my home.
    [R2-D2 reaches out and grabs the lamp.
Alas, naughty droid!
    [R2-D2 and Yoda fight for the lamp.
LUKE O R2, let the creature have it now.   110
    [R2-D2 releases the lamp.
Now move along, good fellow. We have much
To do. Thou art small in both size and help.
YODA Nay, nay, I shall stay.
For I shall stay and help thee
Find thy long lost friend.   115
LUKE Thou dost not understand, thou useless scamp.
I search not for a friend in this damp place,
But for a Jedi master wise in skill!
YODA O Jedi master!

	Yoda that you seek it is.	120
	'Tis truly Yoda!	
LUKE	[*aside:*] A strange turn of events! This tiny sprite	
	May yet prove useful if he knows the man.	
	[*To Yoda:*] Attend: thou know'st of Yoda, little one?	
YODA	I'll take thee to him.	125
	Aye, but first, let us eat food.	
	Come, I good food have!	
LUKE	I follow. R2, stay and watch the camp—	
	Mayhap some hope still lives within this damp.	

[Exeunt, Luke following Yoda.

ACT III

SCENE 1.

Aboard the Millennium Falcon, *inside the asteroid.*

Enter HAN SOLO, PRINCESS LEIA, CHEWBACCA, *and* C-3PO.

HAN   Now shall I shut down ev'rything except
             The ship's emergency pow'r systems.

C-3PO   —Sir,
             I am almost afraid to ask, but doth
             This mean that I shall be shut down as well?

HAN   Nay, nay, good droid, for thou shalt speak unto   5
             The *Falcon* to determine wherefore doth
             The hyperdrive not operate aright.
             For once I find thee useful, goldenrod.
                  [The ship shakes and all are rocked from side to side.

C-3PO   Sir, it is possible this ast'roid may
             Not be entirely stable.

HAN   —Dost thou think?   10
             O droid of wisdom, skill, and excellence—
             Howe'er would I survive if I did not
             Have thee here to reveal such mysteries?
             From usefulness to obvious within
             A single stroke. I pray, Chewbacca, take   15
             This scholar made of wires and metal to
             The back and plug him in the hyperdrive!

C-3PO   Sometimes I do not comprehend the strange
             And varied ways of human beings. True
             It is that I did only try to help!   20
                       [Exeunt Chewbacca and C-3PO. The ship
                       shakes again and Leia falls into Han's arms.

LEIA   [*aside:*] O happy accident! O fall most fair!
            Now in his arms, where I have long'd to be,
            I know not whether 'tis the ship or if
            It is my heart that I feel quaking. Yet,
            Alas, this moment not befits our love.   25
            The situation is too strain'd. I wish,
            With all my being, to be in this place—
            But not like this. [*To Han:*] Pray, let me go.

HAN   —Tut, tut!

LEIA   I prithee, let me go.

HAN   [*aside:*]   —O small request
            That tears apart my soul! [*To Leia:*] Indeed, indeed,   30
            Be not with such excitement overcome.

LEIA   My captain, being held by you is far
            Too plain a thing to e'er excite my mood.

HAN   I crave your kindly pardon, sweetheart fierce,
            But we have little time for something else—   35
            I'll leave thee here alone and then, mayhap,
            The time apart shall heighten thy desire.

                                        [*Exit Han Solo.*

LEIA   O man of pride and will most obstinate!
            However can I love thee, being as
            You are? But being other than you are,   40
            I would not love thee. How this pirate hath
            Laid claim upon the bounty of my soul!
            O, wherefore did I speak so testily?
            Why is it that whenever he is near
            My wit is turn'd to unto a laser beam   45
            With Han plac'd firmly in its sights? I tear
            His heart in twain with words too cruel and harsh,
            Then wonder why he is so full of pride.

'Tis now quite clear that he with arrogance
Doth speak so that he may his heart protect.   50
Forsooth, was e'er a woman placèd in
So delicate a situation yet?

                                [*Exit Princess Leia.*

Enter C-3PO.

C-3PO   O, where is that knave R2 now? For when
        I need him most, then is he far away.
        Perhaps on some adventure, which will serve   55
        To puff him up most mightily, and leave
        Him ever bragging o'er his exploits. Pish!
        The scrawny, errant scamp perplexes me,
        For he is both my nuisance and delight—
        The thorn deep in my side and, stranger still,   60
        The very object of my happiness.

Enter HAN SOLO *and* CHEWBACCA.

        Now, Captain Solo, pray, a word with thee.
HAN   [*aside:*] A word from thee belike means hundreds more.
C-3PO   I know not where your ship did learn to speak—
        It hath a most peculiar dialect.   65
        It is as though 'twere programm'd by a thief,
        And spends its days with smugglers, thugs, and crooks.
        But now, no more of that; my point is made.
        It doth report the power coupling on
        The axis negative is polariz'd,   70
        And must replacèd be to operate.
HAN   'Tis plain it must replacèd be. Presume

Thou not to tell a pilot—one so grand
As me, at least—the bus'ness of his ship.

[*Exit C-3PO.*

[*To Chewbacca:*] Good Chewie?

CHEWBAC.   —Egh?

HAN   —It seems we must replace   75
The power coupling negative, yes?

CHEWBAC.   —Grrm.

[*Exit Chewbacca.*

Enter PRINCESS LEIA, *aside, working.*

HAN   [*aside:*] We are alone. Yet ev'ry time I have
Approach'd her recently I've been rebuff'd.
This should not be a nut I cannot crack—
I am not ignorant in women's ways.   80
Although, by troth, most often when I speak
Of "she" or "her," I indicate my ship.
And yet, I am a man of many strengths:
I pilot ships with talent, skill, and grace,
In battles or in races hard to best,   85
My swift maneuvers legendary are
And through the galaxy my ship is known.
But with this princess, all my skill is naught.
My tongue is tied, and I resort to barbs
And witticisms sloppily convey'd.   90
How shall I show this princess my true heart?
How set aside my ego and be kind?
Here, in this moment, I shall undertake
To set my pathway not toward my pride,
But through the smoother course that runs to love.   95

[*He approaches to help her and is shoved away.*

[*To Leia:*] Pray patience, Worship, I but try to help!

LEIA   Couldst thou forswear thy pompous attitude
And promise thou shalt ne'er call me that name?

HAN   Aye, Leia.

LEIA   [*aside:*]   —Prithee, give me patience now!
To make him thine, respond thou not with fire.   100
[*To Han:*] You do not make it simple.

HAN   —Yes, 'tis true.
But 'tis not I alone who is to blame,
For thou couldst softer and more gentle be.
O Princess, may we end these pointless games?
May we two souls of flame extinguish'd be   105
Just long enough to drink of love's rewards?
I ask thee, truly, dost thou sometimes think
That certain virtues may be found in me?
Canst thou imagine ever looking deep
Into my soul to see the man within?   110
[*Leia stops working and rubs her sore hands.*

LEIA   Occasionally, mayhap, when you are
Not acting in the manner of a scoundrel.
[*Han Solo takes Leia's hands in his.*

HAN   A scoundrel? "Scoundrel" is the word you choose?
I like that word, when spoken from your lips.

LEIA   Pray cease that touch, it doth my heart confuse.   115

HAN   But wherefore cease? What reason shall eclipse
The greater reason of my heart's intent?

LEIA   But lo, my hands are dirtied by my work.

HAN   My hands are likewise dirty. Pray, assent
Unto this moment. What fear makes you shirk?   120

LEIA   What fear? I tell thee, I am not afraid.

HAN   Did I imagine that your hands did shake?
     Thou likest that I am of scoundrel made.
     For thy life could more scoundrel gladly take.
     If thou wouldst cast my suit off, think again— 125
     I would that thou within me deeper look.
LEIA   I tell thee true, that I do like nice men.
HAN   I too am nice.

                    [They kiss.

        Enter C-3PO.

LEIA   *[aside:]*   —He kisses by the book.
C-3PO Sir, Sir, I've isolated the reverse
     Flux power coupling. Have I done thee proud? 130

               [Exit Princess Leia.

HAN	O thank you, 3PO, thank you so much.
C-3PO	But speak none of it, Sir—I have a touch.

[*Exeunt.*

SCENE 2.

Aboard the Empire's Super Star Destroyer.

Enter DARTH VADER *and* CAPTAIN NEEDA *(in beam).*

NEEDA   The swift *Millenn'um Falcon* made its way
               Unto the field of asteroids and that,
               My great Lord Vader, was the last that they
               Within our scopes did e'er appear. They must
               Have been destroy'd, if one considers all   5
               The damage we have tolerated here.
VADER   Your answer's insufficient, Captain, for
               I know they are alive. Thy scanners are
               Poor proxies for the Force. Now listen well
               To my command: I tell thee ev'ry ship   10
               That hath some power left to give shall search
               The ast'roid field until they have been found.
NEEDA   I shall with haste fulfill thy shrewd decree.

[*Exit Captain Needa from beam.*

Enter ADMIRAL PIETT.

PIETT   My Lord?
VADER   —Yes, Admiral?
PIETT   —The Emperor
               Commands that thou do contact him at once.   15

VADER   Then, move the ship out of the ast'roid field
           That I may with my master clearly speak.
PIETT   We will, my Lord.

                              [*Exit Admiral Piett.*

VADER   —Now shall I speak with my
           Dread Emperor. The man who gave me life
           When all was lost. The man to whom I owe   20
           All that I am, and e'er shall be. The man,
           Indeed, who like a father is to me.
           His plans for pow'r and schemes most excellent
           I do obey and carry out with pride.
           Though people fear my aspect bleak and dark,   25
           They should, more surely, fear what I will do
           When answering his perfect, flawless will.
           For sooner would I sacrifice my life
           Than disobey the word of this great man.

                Enter EMPEROR PALPATINE, *in beam.*

           What is thy bidding, master pure and true?   30
EMPEROR   There is a great disturbance in the Force.
VADER   I too have felt it.
EMPEROR   —A new enemy
           Arises, e'en the rebel who destroy'd
           The Death Star—and I have no doubt this boy
           Is kin to Anakin Skywalker.
VADER   [*aside:*]   —O,   35
           Profoundest revelation! I knew he
           Was powerful and bore Skywalker's name,
           Yet that the boy is kin to Anakin
           I did not see. [*To the Emperor:*] How is this possible?

EMPEROR   You only must within your feelings search,   40
            Lord Vader. Then shalt thou too know 'tis true.
            He could destroy us.
VADER   —He is but a boy,
            And Obi-Wan no longer is his help.
EMPEROR   The Force is strong with him, and mark me well:
            The son of Skywalker must ne'er become   45
            A Jedi. Dost thou comprehend my words?
VADER   [aside:] I do his meaning understand, and yet
            Another future for this boy I'll write.
            Not death, but something even greater still.
            It may be that this young Skywalker will   50
            Still prove to be most worthy of the name.
            [To the Emperor:] If he could but be turn'd, an ally
                                                   strong
            He could become.
EMPEROR   —Indeed, thou speakest true.
            The boy may prove himself an asset sure.
            Can it be done? What is thy true reply?   55
VADER   The boy shall surely join us, or shall die.
                                              [Exeunt.

SCENE 3.

Inside Yoda's homestead.

Enter LUKE SKYWALKER.

LUKE   This creature I have follow'd to his home,
            But still no further answers are reveal'd.
            It seemeth that he stalls in bringing me

Unto the one I truly hope to see.
With all that hath befallen in this place   5
My patience runneth thin. I'll press the point.

Enter YODA.

Thy generosity is truly rare,
I'll warrant that thy food delicious is.
Yet neither rhyme nor reason have I heard
Of wherefore we may not go, even now,   10
To see good Master Yoda where he lives.

YODA   Pray, patience, young one.
           For Jedi too must eat—thus
           My good food, eat now.

LUKE   How many leagues away is Yoda? Shall   15
           The journey to him long and per'lous be?

YODA   Not far is Yoda.
           Aye, soon thou shalt be with him.
           First, eat of rootleaf.

           Feast for a Jedi—   20
           Food that enlivens the mind
           Should thy repast be.

           And now, a question:
           What drives the young man's heart to
           Learn the Jedi way?   25

LUKE   This is an inquiry perceptive, friend,
           For I am driv'n by force unto the Force:
           My noble father doth inform my steps.

YODA   Thy father, indeed.

                    Powerful Jedi was he.   30
                    Powerful Jedi.
LUKE   Avaunt, thou silly creature, how canst thou
                    My father know? For surely thou dost not
                    E'en know who I am. Fie! I know not what
                    Or who or why or when or where or how   35
                    Hath brought about this meeting! Time is short;
                    Each minute pass'd with thee hath gone to waste!
YODA   [*speaking to the air:*] I cannot teach him.
                    The boy hath none of patience.
                    How shall he be taught?   40

        The voice of the GHOST OF OBI-WAN KENOBI *is heard.*

OBI-WAN   He patience lacks, but patience can be learn'd.
YODA   Much anger in him.
                    Sudden and quick in quarrel:
                    Too like his father.
OBI-WAN   Was I then diff'rent when thou didst teach me?   45
YODA   He is not ready.
                    'Tis now the thing that I see:
                    This one's unprepar'd.
LUKE   'Tis Yoda! Nay, but Ben, pray argue for
                    My cause, for verily prepar'd am I!   50
                    I can and shall a Jedi be. True, Ben?
YODA   Ready are you, hmm?
                    What know you yet of ready?
                    Say naught of "ready."

                    For eight hundred years   55
                    Have I the Jedi trainèd,

So say not "ready."

I my own counsel
Shall keep on who's to be trained!
A Jedi is wise.   60

A strong commitment
And a most serious mind
Are necessary.

Long have I watch'd him.
All his life looking away   65
To the future, hmm,

To the horizon.
Ne'er his mind on where he was,
What he was doing!

Ventures, excitement: 70
A Jedi craveth not these.
Thou art reckless, aye!

OBI-WAN   And so was I, if thou dost think on it.
YODA   And he is too old
            The training to begin now.   75
            Certain, he's too old.
LUKE   But Master Yoda, I have learn'd so much.
YODA   And will he finish
            The thing he doth begin here?
            I prithee, tell me.   80
LUKE   I shall not fail thee: 'tis my promise true,
            For I am not afraid of anything.

YODA   Thou shalt be yet, Luke.
                My words most carefully heed:
                Thou shalt be, indeed.   85

[Exeunt.

SCENE 4.

Aboard the Millennium Falcon, *inside the asteroid.*

Enter HAN SOLO, CHEWBACCA, *and* C-3PO.

C-3PO   Good Sir, if I may venture my belief—
HAN   I tell thee honestly, C-3PO,
                That neither appetite nor inclination
                Have I to feast upon your odd beliefs.
                Do thou thy work but keep opinion out,   5
                And we shall feast together on the silence.

Enter PRINCESS LEIA, *in fear.*

LEIA   O Han, a horrid sight I have just seen!
                Whilst I did in the cockpit sit and think—
HAN   On what? Pray tell: what didst thou think upon?
LEIA   'Tis not the time for jokes and parries, please!   10
                As I did sit there, suddenly a jolt
                Went through me as I heard a sound upon
                The window. Looking closer, I espied
                A second beast outside that hard upon
                The window fell. There's something out there,
                                  Han—   15
        Beyond the ship, abiding in the cave.

[*A great sound is heard and the ship shakes.*

CHEWBAC.   Auugh!

C-3PO   —Listen!

HAN   —I shall venture out to see.

LEIA   Nay, art thou mad? It is not wise or safe
           To go without when there are creatures we
           Know nothing of.

HAN   —This bucket is just fix'd,   20
           Wouldst thou I let some thing tear it apart?

LEIA   I see thy reason, and shall go with thee.

C-3PO   I shall with courage and with honor stay
           Behind to bravely guard the ship.

                                [*Another sound is heard.*
                            O dear!
                    [*Exit C-3PO as the others go outside the ship.*

LEIA   What is this ground that we do walk upon?   25
           'Tis strange—it doth not feel at all like rock.

HAN   Indeed, with thine assessment I agree:
           It seems there is much moisture in this place.

LEIA   I have a feeling bad about this cave.
           What odd new situation find we here?   30
           Do not these signs and portents give thee fear?

HAN   Aye.

                                [*Han sees something move.*
                    Take thou cover!

                                        [*He shoots.*
                            'Tis all right.

LEIA   —What is't?

HAN   'Tis what I did suspect: some mynocks. They
           Are fasten'd to the ship, a'chewing on
           The power cables.

LEIA   —Mynocks? O what beasts!   35

HAN   Return inside, and we shall search for more.

> *[Several mynocks fly by. Han shoots,*
> *and the cave walls shake.*

But hold one moment, something seems awry,
For blaster fire should not cause walls to shake.

> *[Han shoots the cave wall,*
> *and the ground shakes mightily.*

O, horror, for I now do understand:
The cave doth quake whenever it is shot.   40
But what knows rock of pain, or stone of hurt?
Whenever did a cave feel anything?
Impossible it is, unless this cave
Is much more than a cave. [*To Leia and Chewbacca:*]

> Pray, go inside!
> *[They run into the* Millennium Falcon.

With speed now, Chewie, let us fly away!   45

LEIA   *[following Han to the cockpit:]* The Empire is without,
we should not go—

HAN   We've no time to discuss this in committee.

LEIA   O, fie! Thou scoundrel, I am no committee!

> *[They arrive in the cockpit and start the ship.*

See reason! For thou canst not make the jump
To lightspeed midst this field of asteroids.   50

HAN   Make sure thy back end finds a seat—we go!

> *[They begin to leave the cave, which is actually an*
> *exogorth, or space slug. Its mouth begins to close.*

Enter C-3PO.

C-3PO   Observe! We are destroy'd!

HAN	—I see it plain.
C-3PO	O, we are doom'd!
LEIA	—The cave, it doth collapse!
HAN	This is no cave, and I am not its food.
	Now we do fly—another close escape! 55

       [Exeunt C-3PO, Han Solo, Princess Leia, and
          Chewbacca in the Milennium Falcon, *flying out*
          of exogorth's mouth and leaving it alone on stage.

EXOGOR.	Alas, another meal hath fled and gone,
	And in the process I am sorely hurt.
	These travelers who have escap'd my reach
	Us'd me past the endurance of a block!
	My stomach they did injure mightily 60
	With jabs and pricks, as though a needle were

A'bouncing in my belly. O cruel Fate!
To be a space slug is a lonely lot,
With no one on this rock to share my life,
No true companion here to mark my days.   65
And now my meals do from my body fly—
Was e'er a beast by supper so abus'd?
Was e'er a creature's case so pitiful?
Was e'er an exogorth as sad as I?
Was e'er a tragedy as deep as mine?   70
I shall with weeping crawl back to my cave,
Which shall, sans food, belike become my grave.

                                   [Exit.

SCENE 5.

The Dagobah system.

Enter YODA, R2-D2, *and* LUKE SKYWALKER, *training.*

LUKE   [*aside:*] This Yoda is indeed a teacher wise,
                 And hath agreed to train me in the way
                 Of Jedi. Strong and quick I show myself—
                 With leaps and flips I train my body and
                 Instill within a Jedi's discipline.   5
                 Aye, with the Force I like a sand bat fly.
                 My spirit feeleth free, my muscles strong,
                 My mind is calm inside, my heart is still.
                 What gratitude I feel toward this new
                 And treasur'd mentor. Thus I train my best—   10
                 His expectations I'll not disappoint.
YODA   Now run, indeed, run!

A Jedi's strength doth surely
Come from the Force, Luke.

But mind the dark side.   15
Anger, fear, aggression—from
The dark side are they.

Easily they flow,
Quick to join you in a fight.
Aye, they do not fail!   20

Once on the dark path,
Forever shall it control
Thy destiny, Luke.

It shall consume thee,
As it did the apprentice   25
Of good Obi-Wan.

LUKE   Darth Vader: legendary is his pow'r.
           But Master, hath the dark side greater strength?

YODA   Nay, nay—forsooth: nay.
           'Tis quicker, easier, more   30
           Seductive only.

LUKE   But how, good master, shall I know the good
           Side from the bad, the darkness from the light?

YODA   Thou shalt know, my lad,
           When thou art calm and passive.   35
           [*Aside:*] I hope thou shalt know.

When fac'd with terror,
And with thy father's grim fate,

I hope thou shalt know.

[*To Luke:*] A Jedi uses   40
The Force only for knowledge
And defense. Is't clear?

The Force is no club,
Neither is it a weapon
Us'd for attacking.   45

LUKE   Yet it is still a weapon for defense.
              So wherefore may I not the Force employ—
YODA   Nay, there's no wherefore.
              Nothing more shall come today.
              From thy questions, rest.   50
LUKE   [*aside:*] Reliev'd am I this training to complete,
              If only for this day, which hath been years.
              But is this not a strange and troubling thing?
              Where only moments past I felt at ease,
              Now there's some sprite within that troubles me— 55
              A chill, a solemn aura in my bones.
              I would not much ado o'er nothing make,
              But still shall I ask Yoda what it is.
              [*To Yoda:*] I feel a cold, a presage here of death.
              What is it that I sense within this place?   60
                        [*Yoda points to the opening of a cave.*
YODA   With the Force's dark side
              Is that place yonder quite strong.
              A place of evil.

              Discover thou shalt

That wherever good is found,   65
Evil is nearby.

Here on Dagobah
'Tis also so. For e'en here
That evil place is.

Bound thou art now, Luke,   70
To enter it, and face its
Deepest darknesses.

LUKE   But Sir, I prithee, tell me: what's within?

YODA   Only that which thou
Shalt take away with thee, Luke.   75

[Luke begins to enter the cave,
carrying his weapons.

Take not thy weapons.

R2-D2   Beep, meep, meep, squeak, beep, whistle, meep,
beep, nee!

[Luke enters, bringing his weapons,
as Yoda and R2-D2 remain outside.

LUKE   What twists of knotted vines and tangl'd fates
Await me in this hole? I shall go in,
And prove that I am not afraid of it,   80
Nor any task or misadventure here.
What evil can await I have not seen?
For I have facèd evil enemies
Who kill'd my mentor and my family.
What evil in this place can greater be?   85
Now doth time seem to slowly beat its pace.
And all is like a thick and restless dream.
But wait, who comes unto this deep, dark place?

It moves with grace—is it my father good?

Enter shadow of DARTH VADER.

Nay, nay, how I have been deceiv'd, abus'd!   90
For it is Vader here, my greatest foe,
The cruel defiler of my father's youth.
I stand preparèd to do battle as
A Jedi, full of rage and righteous hate.
Now up, lightsaber, light my keen revenge!   95
Lay on, Darth Vader, damnèd henchman vile.
And now we fight! Yet seems it that my limbs
Are made of stone—but he is slower still!
I see my chance to strike, and let it fall—
The blow that shall release my father's soul.   100
Now Vader's head doth fall onto the ground
And I feel no relief, but only pain.
The mask doth split, his visage to reveal!
O, I shall see the face that kill'd a man,
That kill'd a thousand fathers like my own.   105
But wait, what is this here—and can it be?
This is no face of Vader: 'tis my face!
The horror, O the horror! Darker yet
That e'er I had imagin'd possible.
The greatest evil I may face—myself!   110
                              [Exit Luke, in fear.

YODA   Now hath he seen it,
              And he shall ever see it
              Till he sees it through.

                              [Exit Yoda.

R2-D2   O strange and somber night that falleth here—

My master Luke all out of sorts from what   115
He spies inside this hole. What lesson is
It Yoda hath reveal'd to him inside?
I would that I my master could protect,
But such is not the role I have to play.
And thus, since I may not protector be,   120
My path shall be to play the fool and watch:
I shall maintain my droidlike silence and
Bear witness as the boy becomes the man,
The learner doth become the Jedi true.
Content yourself with this, R2, and rest,   125
For other times than these require your best.

                                      [Exit.

SCENE 6.

*Space, aboard the Empire's Super Star Destroyer
and the* Millennium Falcon.

Enter ADMIRAL PIETT *and* IMPERIAL CONTROLLER, *with* DARTH VADER
and BOUNTY HUNTERS, *including* BOBA FETT, *aside,
aboard the Super Star Destroyer.*

PIETT   These bounty hunters, O they reek! We have
               No need for their most wretched scum.
CONTROL.   —Aye, Sir.
PIETT   The rebels surely shall not 'scape us now.
CONTROL.   We have been hail'd by the *Avenger* ship.
PIETT   Now let us hear it.
VADER   —There shall be rewards   5
               Aplenty for the one who finds the swift

Millenn'um Falcon. Ye may use whate'er
Approaches, weapons, means, or what ye will,
But mark ye well: I want them all alive.
[*To Boba Fett:*] There shall be no disintegrations.
                                                     Clear?   10

FETT   As you wish. [*Aside:*] The darkest Sith that e'er
              did live, and I am his choice to find those he cannot.
              Yet who am I? A mere bounty hunter like the others
              here? Nay, far more. I am Boba Fett, the vilest,
              fiercest, most deadly hunter in the galaxy. More   15
              than that, Darth Vader knows that I shall serve
              him well and faithfully in the pursuit of Solo. He
              knoweth well that Boba Fett doth worship at sweet
              compensation's throne, and would happily
              betray my own kin to earn the great reward   20
              that hath been promis'd. I would kill Solo
              without a thought, for what is he to me?

Disintegrations, indeed. I would disintegrate,
disembowel, dismember, destroy utterly Han Solo,
for I know him not nor care what he hath done　25
to earn Darth Vader's ire and the scorn of Jabba
of the Hutt. I shall play my bounty hunter's part,
obey the dark lord, take my prize from the Empire,
and receive a second prize on the dunes of Tatooine.
A double prize—'tis wonderful a bounty hunter to be.　30

PIETT　[*to Darth Vader:*] My Lord, the ship hath been
　　　　　　　　　　　　　　　　discoverèd!

[*Exeunt Darth Vader, Boba Fett, other bounty hunters,*
　　　Admiral Piett, and Imperial Controller.

Enter HAN SOLO, CHEWBACCA, PRINCESS LEIA,
　　and C-3PO *aboard the* Millennium Falcon.

C-3PO　O, praise the maker! We are venturing
　　　　Out of the ast'roid field, and are alive—
　　　　Miraculous! [*Aside:*] I almost am convinc'd
　　　　That Captain Solo bears a hero's air.　35

HAN　Now let us hence. Chewbacca, art prepar'd
　　　For lightspeed?

CHEWBAC.　　　—Auugh!

HAN　　　　　—Now one, two, three, and go!
　　　　　[*The* Millennium Falcon *makes a sound and fails.*

CHEWBAC.　Egh.

HAN　　　—'Tis not fair. I say, it is not just!

C-3PO　[*aside:*] A hero, did I say? O man of folly!

CHEWBAC.　Auugh, auugh!

HAN　　　　　—The transfer circuits do not work　40
　　　'Tis not my fault!

LEIA   —No lightspeed once again?

HAN   'Tis not my fault. In troth, 'tis not my fault!

C-3PO   The rear deflector shield is compromis'd,
             And if we do sustain another hit
             Upon the ship's back quarter, 'tis our end.   45

HAN   [*aside:*] 'Tis madness, this maneuver I'll attempt.
             But desp'rate times for desp'rate measures call.
             [*To Chewbacca:*] Turn thou this ship around.

CHEWBAC.   —Egh?

HAN   —Turn it 'round!
             I shall put all our pow'r to shields in front.

LEIA   Thou wilt attack a Star Destroyer?

C-3PO   —Sir!   50
             The odds of our success in a direct
             Attack upon a Star Destroyer—

LEIA   —Tut!
                [*Exeunt, flying toward the Star Destroyer.*

Enter CAPTAIN NEEDA, TRACKING OFFICER,
and COMMUNICATIONS OFFICER.

NEEDA   They move into attack position—shields!
             But now, where are they gone? Pray, track them straight.

TRACK.   The ship's no longer shown in any scopes.   55

NEEDA   That is impossible. No ship that small
             Hath any ways or means to cloak itself.
             Nay, they cannot, as magic, disappear.

COMM.   Good Captain Needa, our Lord Vader doth
             Demand an update of our keen pursuit.   60

NEEDA   [*aside:*] O dreaded moment. This shall mean my death.
             Farewell now, for my life's gone with the ship.

[*To Communications Officer:*] Prepare a shuttle for me.
                                    I'll accept
The full responsibility for their
Escape, and shall apologize unto
Lord Vader. Keep thy watch most vigilant.   65

COMM.   Aye, Captain Needa.
                    [*Exit Tracking and Communications officers.*

               Enter DARTH VADER, *as Captain Needa
                    makes his way toward him.*

NEEDA   —On thy mercy great
I throw myself and all my hopes, dear lord.
The great *Millenn'um Falcon* now is fled.
It hath evaded even our vast fleet.   70
Take my apology—

VADER   —The ship is lost?
And thus thy life—dead for a ducat, dead!
                    [*Darth Vader chokes Captain
                    Needa with the Force, killing him.*
The necks of fools deserve a crushing Force.
Let this serve as thy dying lesson, Needa.
With that last breath thy recompense is done   75
And all apologies accepted.

               Enter ADMIRAL PIETT.

PIETT   —Lord,
Our scan of the surrounding area
Is now complete, but has, alas, found naught.
Lord, if the swift *Millenn'um Falcon* hath

Made good the jump to lightspeed, it may be   80
Beyond the far end of the galaxy.

VADER   Alert thou every Imperi'l post,
And calculate the ship's most likely course
From its trajectory as it did flee.

PIETT   Aye, Lord, I'll warrant we shall find them soon.   85

[Exit Admiral Piett.

VADER   O ancestors, pray save me from these fools
Who with their instruments and scanners could
Not find a bantha in a womp rat's hole.
But calm thyself now, Vader, be at ease.
This momentary failure may yet prove   90
Most beneficial, and I'll warrant that
The time shall not go dully by us, for
It shall be us'd to finalize my plans
And think upon the moment when I shall
Both meet and then defeat the Skywalker   95
Who dares to call the Empire enemy.
So let these rebels go for now, my soul,
And ponder how to make their downfall whole.

[Exit.

SCENE 7.

The Dagobah system.

Enter YODA, R2-D2, *and* LUKE SKYWALKER, *who practices
lifting things with the Force.*

YODA   Use the Force, Luke, yes.
Now, lift thou the stone. Feel it.

The Force within flows.
              [R2-D2 begins to beep as Luke's ship sinks.
Nay, listen thou not
To the droid and all his beeps.   5
Do thou concentrate!
              [Everything that was lifted falls.

R2-D2   Nee, nee, beep, meep, beep, squeak, squeak,
                          whistle, squeak!

LUKE   Fie! We shall never extricate the ship.

YODA   So certain are you?
Always with you, my pupil,   10
It cannot be done.

What have we done here—
Hear'st thou nothing that I say?
Dost thou attend, Luke?

If depend upon   15
The Force thou shalt, anything
Possible shall be.

LUKE   But Master, moving stones with the great Force
I do admit may be achiev'd. But this,
This ship—to lift its hulk, its mass, its size—   20
'Tis different, aye, wholly different!

YODA   Nay! No different.
Only within thy mind, Luke,
Different it is.

Thou must unlearn all   25
Those things that thou hast learnèd.
Dost thou understand?

LUKE   In troth, I understand, and I shall try.

YODA   Nay, nay! Try thou not.
            But do thou or do thou not,   30
            For there is no "try."

LUKE   [*aside:*] I shall stretch out my mind, and shall attempt,
            But this is madness—lifting e'en a ship?
            The greatest Jedi still cannot achieve
            That which is patently impossible.   35
            Methinks no Force can move this ship, and thus
            I certain am I never shall do this.

                        [*Luke tries to lift the ship with the Force,*
                            but the ship sinks lower.

R2-D2   Beep, hoo.

LUKE   —Nay, I cannot. 'Tis much too big.

YODA   Nay, size matters not.
            Look thou at me, I prithee.   40
            Judge me by my size?

            And where you should not.
            For my ally 'tis the Force.
            A pow'rful ally.

            Life doth create it.   45
            Its energy surrounds us,
            Binds us together.

            Luminous beings
            We are, not this crude matter.
            You must feel the Force.   50

            All around thee, here—

Between thou and me, tree, rock:
Ev'rywhere it is.

E'en between the land
And your ever-sinking ship,　　　　　　　　　　55
The Force is there, too.

LUKE　　I know now thou dost ask th'impossible.
　　　　　　　　　　[Luke sits aside, as Yoda lifts his hands.

YODA　　[*aside:*] Be mindful, young one,
And watch what inner strength great
May come from small size.　　　　　　　　　　60
　　　　　　　　　　[Yoda moves the ship out of the swamp
　　　　　　　　　　　　　　　　using the Force.

LUKE　　The ship! It cometh out—thou hast done it!
I ne'er imagin'd it was possible.
With eyes I see, but mind does not believe.

YODA　　Thus is your error.
Against the Force you do rail;　　　　　　　　65
That is why you fail.
　　　　　　　　　　　　　　[Exeunt.

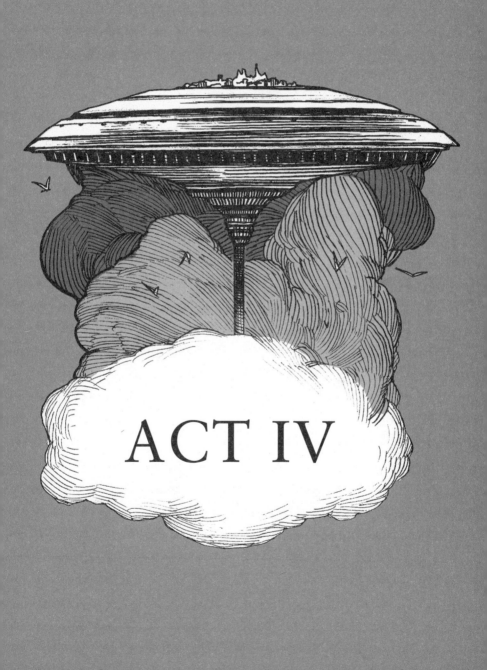

ACT IV

SCENE 1.

Aboard the Millennium Falcon, *moored to a Star Destroyer.*

Enter CHORUS.

CHORUS   With such deep wit Han hath the Empire trick'd
              That now the Falcon hides within its fleet!
              With skill he doth the Empire's moves predict,
              And bravely plans to make his move discreet.

                                                    [Exit.

Enter HAN SOLO, PRINCESS LEIA, CHEWBACCA, *and* C-3PO.

C-3PO   I tell thee, Captain Solo, thou hast gone   5
              Beyond all measure with this reckless move.
              Thou hast put all aboard in danger grave,
              And yet thou seem'st to have but little care.
CHEWBAC.   Auugh!
C-3PO   —Nay, I'll not be silent! Wherefore am
              I never listen'd to?
HAN   —The fleet doth break   10
              Itself up into pieces. [*To Chewbacca:*] Go thee now,
              Chewbacca; stand aside the manual
              Release to liberate the landing claw.
CHEWBAC.   Egh.
                                          [Exit Chewbacca.
C-3PO   —Truly, I see not how that shall help.
              Surrender is, in circumstances such   15
              As these, a fair alternative. Perhaps
              The Empire may yet reasonable be.
                                      [Leia turns off C-3PO.

HAN	Great thanks I give thee for the gift of peace.
LEIA	Brave soul, what dost thou think thou next shalt do?
HAN	Before these ships do from the fleet release, 20
	They should their garbage dump ere they pursue
	A jump to lightspeed. Then we'll float away.
LEIA	Thy ship with all the garbage, eh? Well said.
	And what then?
HAN	—We shall haply find our way
	Unto a port where safety makes its bed. 25
	Pray, dost thou know of any port like such?
LEIA	Mayhap I might, if I knew where we were.
HAN	Anoat system, but doth that help much?
LEIA	O, the Anoat system? I aver:
	'Tis bleak.
HAN	—But hark! An interesting name 30
	My ship's computer showeth: Lando!
LEIA	—Han?
	What Lando system?
HAN	—"System," you exclaim?
	He is not system: Lando is a man.
	As Lando of Calrissian he's known.
	The man doth deal in cards, in gambling and 35
	In scoundreling—thou wouldst his type condone.
LEIA	[aside:] He jests with me as one in love's command!
HAN	He is in Bespin—rather far, but we
	May make it there.
LEIA	[reading from screen:] —A colony? A mine?
HAN	Tibanna gas mine—I would wager he 40
	Hath ta'en the mine that someone did call "mine."
	This Lando hath a hist'ry long with me.
LEIA	But dost thou trust him?

HAN   —Nay, thou'rt right. But I
              Believe we have no need of fear, for he
              No love doth harbor for the Empire, aye.   45
                                        [The ship shakes.
              [*Into comlink:*] Prepare now, Chewie, 'tis the time.
                                                Detach!
                                [The Millennium Falcon *detaches*
                                        from the Star Destroyer.
LEIA   Thou hast these moments that are unsurpass'd—
              Aye, when thou hast them, they are without match.
              Not numerous are they, but aye: thou hast.
                          [Leia kisses Han and exits with C-3PO.
HAN   'Tis said that sometimes those who knew us in   50
              Our youth did know us best. From them we have
              No secrets and cannot pretend to be
              Another thing than what we are. They keep
              Our living honest, for they know who we
              Have been. And such a man is Lando. He   55
              And I have known each other many years,
              So he doth know me from my smuggling past,
              The days when I did gamble, cheat, and fight—
              And often in that order, too. He knew
              Me ere I was with the Rebellion join'd,   60
              And knoweth what Han Solo once hath been.
              Thus is he prim'd uniquely to give aid
              Unto a friend who now hath found a cause:
              A cause to join, a cause e'en to defend.
              O Lando, all our hopes are pinn'd on thee.   65
              What shall it be, old friend? I here take all
              I have—my ship, my mates, my one true love—
              And stake it all on thee and on our past.

How shalt thou answer, O Calrissian?
Will this, my wager, prove a foolish bet?   70
How shall the deck unfold, the players end?
And is the dealing in my favor stack'd?
The playing of the game is yet to be,
But Lando: I do seek to win with thee.

                                                       [Exit.

Enter BOBA FETT.

FETT   A smuggler's ways are e'er unchanging and   75
          predictable. Thou hast let the *Millennium Falcon*
          go out with the refuse, Solo, but I refuse to let
          thee play a jade's trick and go thy merry way.
          Thy course shall I pursue, and e'en best, for my
          ship is swift of flight unlike thy tir'd and agèd   80
          Falcon. To the last I'll grapple with thee, and
          in the heart of Bespin make thee cold with fright.
          The Fett doth promise it, and it shall be.

                                                [Exit Boba Fett.

SCENE 2.

The Dagobah system.

Enter YODA, R2-D2, *and* LUKE SKYWALKER,
doing a handstand and lifting things with the Force.

YODA   Now, concentrate, Luke.
          Feel the Force, how it doth flow.
          Be calm, at peace, yes.

When you use the Force,
The Force, in your soul, begins   5
New paths to open.

Through the Force, your mind
Shall see future things, things past.
Friends nearer and yon.

LUKE   Alas, my mind doth see—'tis Leia, Han!   10
    [Everything drops as Luke's concentration breaks.

YODA   Nay, be in control!
Thou must, beyond all else, Luke,
Have control entire.

LUKE   O vision most horrendous and most drear.
A city in the clouds most beautiful,   15
Beneath a golden sun—as though 'twere heav'n.
But hidden just beneath its luster doth
A harsh and painful nightmare lurk. I saw,
Beneath a sky of orange hues array'd,
Dear Leia weeping at some cruel, dark thing—   20
She will not be consol'd from her great loss.
And Han, his screams do echo in mine ears,
Such cries of suffering I ne'er have heard.
What signs are these, what ghosts of future hurt?
What doth the Force attempt to show to me?   25
O tell me, Master, tell me plain, I pray:
Shall Han and Leia die, is that their fate?

YODA   A future sight, this.
Hard to see is the future—
'Tis e'er in motion.   30

LUKE   I understand 'tis hard for thee to see,
But harder yet the vision echoes in

My head, and reaches deep within my soul.
If thou canst not give reassurance they
Are safe, and shall be safe, 'tis I who must   35
Ensure the same. I will not idly stand
By whilst they suffer many agonies.
My mind is settl'd: I must thither go.

YODA   Decide thou must, how
Thou shalt truly serve them best.   40
Mayhap you may help.

But also shalt thou
Sacrifice all for which they
Shall fight and suffer.

LUKE   But Master, tell me what then I should do?   45
Wouldst thou allow thy friends to suffer thus?
Wouldst thou accept the future's "hard to see"?
Wouldst thou ignore the screams within thy brain?

YODA   [aside:] The boy doth not hear—
His friends' fates I cannot see,   50
But his looketh bleak.

Convince him I must,
Else he shall suffer greatly
And lost is our hope.

[To Luke:] Go not, I prithee.   55
The training must thou complete.
To my words listen!

LUKE   The vision shall not, will not, leave my head.
E'en now I witness Leia in her torment,
And Han, alone, as if upon some isle.   60

E'en brave Chewbacca cries for what is lost—
These signs can only equal tragedy.
They are my friends, and I must fly with haste.
Or else, I'll warrant, all of them may die.

        Enter GHOST OF OBI-WAN KENOBI.

OBI-WAN   Thou canst not know this, Luke. E'en Yoda doth   65
        Not have the pow'r, their final fate to see.
LUKE   But I may help them now; I feel the Force!
OBI-WAN   To see is one thing—to control is yet
        Another. Dangerous this moment is
        For thee, for thou shalt be sore tempted, in   70
        Thy rage, toward the dark side of the Force.

YODA   Yes, to Obi-Wan
              Thou must listen. The cave, Luke:
              Recall thy failure!

LUKE   But truly, I have learn'd so much since then.   75
              I know what I must watch for and beware,
              I know how tempted by the dark I'll be,
              I know this and shall, therefore, guard my soul.
              I tell thee, Master Yoda, I'll return
              And finish all my training. This I vow.   80

OBI-WAN   Pray, open up thine eyes. 'Tis thee and thine
              Abilities the Emperor desires.
              They are the bait, and thou the colo claw—
              Thou art the fish the Emperor would catch.
              Thy friends do suffer only for thy sake,   85
              So that, through them, thou mayst be easily
              Drawn in.

LUKE   —And that is why I have to go.
              Present unto the Emperor the fish,
              And rest assur'd the bait is off the hook.

OBI-WAN   O Luke, I would not lose thee as I lost   90
              Darth Vader. His betrayal made my life
              A bleak and tragic thing. Thy loss unto
              The dark would make my death a hellish, cold
              Eternity.

LUKE   —I shall return, dear Ben.
              My training thus far shall suffice, it is   95
              Enough; I stand prepar'd to face the dark.

YODA   Stoppèd they must be;
              On this depends ev'ry thing.
              But pray, attend me:

Only a fully   100
Trainèd Jedi may defeat
Vader and his Lord.

If thou leavest now,
And here do end thy training,
Thou art choosing ease.   105

And once on the path
Of ease and haste, like Vader
Thou mayst become, Luke.

OBI-WAN   Attend to Yoda's wisdom, Luke, and stay.
            O, exercise thy patience, worthy lad.   110

LUKE   And in the waiting sacrifice my friends?
            Is that the choice that ye would have me make?

YODA   This hard indeed is.
            But if thou honor the thing
            For which they fight: yes.   115

OBI-WAN   If thou dost choose to face Darth Vader, thou
            Shalt be alone; I cannot interfere.

LUKE   I understand, and have been fully warn'd.
            My mind is set; good R2, do prepare.
            Fire up the ship's converters: we depart. 120

OBI-WAN   O, do not give in unto hate, dear Luke,
            In doing so the dark side shalt thou find.
            [*Aside:*] Indeed, I once did see it happen thus.

YODA   Strong is Darth Vader.
            Remember what thou hast learn'd,   125
            For save thee it can.

LUKE   I shall, and shall return: you have my word.
                          [*Exeunt Luke and R2-D2.*

YODA   Warnèd thee I have—
            He a reckless spirit hath.
            Now matters are worse.   130
OBI-WAN   That boy is our first, last, and greatest hope.
                            [Exit Ghost of Obi-Wan Kenobi.
YODA   But nay, 'tis not so.
            For another yet there is:
            One more hope for us.

            O how this plagues me!   135
            The boy for training hath come,
            But too soon is fled.

            A young bird he is,
            Too eager the nest to leave,
            Yet trying to fly.   140

            But young birds fly not—
            Their wings still too fragile are.
            Instead, they do fall.

            And fall this one shall.
            But how far, how fast, how long?   145
            Time only shall tell.

            Little bird, be safe.
            If thou the nest seest again
            I shall meet thee then.
                                              [Exit Yoda.

SCENE 3.
Bespin, the cloud city.

Enter HAN SOLO, CHEWBACCA, PRINCESS LEIA, *and* C-3PO,
attempting to land the Millennium Falcon *in the city,*
speaking with GUARD 1 *in comlink.*

HAN	Nay, nay, good Sir, as I have said before:
	I have no permit that shall let me pass,
	But Lando of Calrissian I seek.
GUARD 1	[*through comlink:*] Thou shalt not enter unto Bespin,
	nay.
HAN	Why dost thou fire at me and my good ship? 5
	Be not so quick to turn to blasters, Sir—
	I prithee, grant me time but to explain . . .
GUARD 1	[*through comlink:*] Make thou no deviation from
	thy course.
C-3PO	These Bespinites are rather petulant—
	They've nothing of my disposition sweet. 10
LEIA	[*to Han:*] I thought that thou didst say thou knowest this
	Man Lando.
CHEWBAC.	—Auugh!
HAN	—But 'twas so long ago.
	Nay, surely he doth hold no grudge by now.
GUARD 1	[*through comlink:*] Thou hast permission now to
	land upon
	The platform three–two–seven.
HAN	—Many thanks. 15
	Now do ye see, ye doubters all? I tell
	Ye truly: Lando is a friend, indeed.
LEIA	Nay, who hath worri'd? [*Aside:*] Verily, there is

A something here that seemeth not aright:
This welcome hath been less than welcoming.   20
Yet Han with brave nobility hath led
Our troubl'd quest—I shall not doubt him now.
          [*The* Millennium Falcon *lands and Han Solo,*
            Chewbacca, Princess Leia, and C-3PO disembark.

CHEWBAC. Egh.

C-3PO   —O, there is no one to meet us here.

LEIA   I do not like this, Han.

HAN   —What wouldst thou like?

C-3PO   At least we are no more upon the ship—   25
Enough of space I've seen to last a life.
'Twas kind of them to let us land.

HAN   [*to Princess Leia:*] —Be calm
And trust me, all things shall end well.

          Enter LANDO *with* LOBOT *and* GUARDS.

                My friend!
[*To Chewbacca:*] But keep thou watch now, Chewie,
                              just in case.

LANDO   [*aside:*] How shall I play this? Shall I distant be?   30
Nay, then he shall become suspicious and
May have some cause to fear ere Vader comes.
I shall be jovial and shine with joy—
A colt is ridden best by kindly rider.
I know 'tis true: it worketh ev'ry time.   35
Thus, to deceive I shall employ a jest.
[*Walking to Han:*] Thou slimy, double-crossing,
                              no-good swine!
Thou hast a nerve to show thy cheating face,

	Since thou hast prov'n thyself a lying thief.	
HAN	Is't possible? Is friendship's mem'ry slain?	40
LANDO	Heigh-ho, I mock at thee, my goodly friend!	
	How art thou, pirate? 'Tis a joy to see	
	Thee here.	
C-3PO	[*to Princess Leia:*] —He doth seem full of	
	friendship's mirth.	
LEIA	Aye, truly, he seems full of it indeed.	
LANDO	What brings thee here to Bespin?	
HAN	—Ship repairs.	45
	Methought thou couldst some kind assistance grant.	
LANDO	What hast thou done unto my ship?	
HAN	—Thy ship?	
	Remember thou didst lose her o'er to me	
	As fairly as the day is long.	
LANDO	—And how	
	Dost thou, Chewbacca? Hang'st thou still around	50
	This aging renegade?	
CHEWBAC.	—Egh!	
LANDO	[*to Princess Leia:*] —O, what light	
	Doth break upon mine eyes? What beauty's this?	
	I give thee welcome, gentle lady. I	
	Am Lando of Calrissian, and do	
	Administer this great facility.	55
	And who, pray tell, art thou? Eh?	
LEIA	—Leia, I.	
LANDO	[*kissing her hand:*] Most welcome, Leia.	
HAN	—Aye, 'tis well, 'tis well.	
	Thou ever wert a lover of fair things.	
C-3PO	C-3PO am I, and at your service . . .	
	[*Lando turns his back.*	

	[*Aside:*] I wonder that I still am talking here:	60
	Nobody marks me.	
LANDO	[*to Han:*] —What doth ail the ship?	
HAN	The hyperdrive.	
LANDO	—My people shall begin	
	Work on't immediately. I tell thee,	
	That ship in many cases sav'd my life!	
	What stories of adventure I could tell	65
	In which the ship doth play the central part.	
	She is the fastest heap of scrap in all	
	The galaxy!	
LEIA	[*aside:*] —He loveth this old ship	
	Almost as much as Han! This love of ships,	
	'Tis like an illness wild within these men.	70
HAN	Now tell me of thy life and bus'ness, friend—	
	How doth the gas mine for thee? Doth it pay?	
LANDO	'Tis credits in and credits out, but more,	

I fear, of out than in. We are but small,
An outpost minor. Thus have I supply   75
Dilemmas, labor difficulties, too.

HAN   Ha, ha!

LANDO   —Why say'st thou "Ha"? And wherefore twice?

HAN   'Tis thou. Pray, hearken unto thine own voice.
So rife with deep responsibility,
So serious, experienc'd, mature,   80
And bus'nesslike. 'Twas not my expectation.

LANDO   [*aside:*] O weep, my heart, to see him brings such joy,
And pains me more to seal his awful fate.
[*To Han:*] Pray, hear me truly, Han. Whatever else
May happen, hear these words: this moment doth   85
Recall for me our past together, which
Is sweetness in my memory.

HAN   —Indeed.
'Tis well to see thee thriving so, my friend.

LANDO   And thou hast hit the mark: I duties bear,
And grave responsibilities are mine.   90
'Tis but the price of one's success, I s'pose.

                    [*Exeunt Han Solo, Chewbacca,
                        Princess Leia, and Lando.*

                Enter another 3PO DROID.

C-3PO   What joy to see a kind, familiar face.

DROID   E chu ta!
                              [*Exit 3PO droid.*

C-3PO   —O, how rude! But pray, what's here?
                         [*C-3PO enters another room.*
Was that an R2 unit's sound I heard?

Is't possible that R2-D2's here?   95
Hello, who is herein?

Enter a SHADOWY FIGURE.

FIGURE   —Say, who art thou?
C-3PO   Alas, this is my end! An enemy—
               If only I could others tell. O me!
                    [Exeunt as C-3PO *is shot into pieces.*

Enter PRINCESS LEIA.

LEIA   Time's passage hath not sooth'd my mind's distress.
              Full many moments we have waited here   100

Within this lovely city in the clouds,
Yet I am neither rested nor relax'd.
Foreboding doth creep o'er me like a plague—
My mind is sore afeard, my hands do shake,
And nowhere can my troubl'd soul find peace.   105
The quick permission given us to land,
The too-familiar welcome Lando gave,
A small apartment offer'd for our use—
It seems as though we were expected here,
Though how this could have happen'd, I know not.   110
For surely when th'Imperi'l fleet broke up,
We in the opposite direction flew.
But e'en beyond that worry there is more,
For though I do not love the prating droid
C-3PO has not been seen since our   115
Arrival here. We have too much of quiet—
I almost miss his constant chattering.

                Enter HAN SOLO.

HAN   All shall be well. The ship is fix'd with care.
            There are but two or three things more, then will
            We make our swift departure hence. 'Tis fair?   120
LEIA   The swiftest shall be best. Some thing is still
            Awry. Where is C-3PO? He hath
            Not seen us or been seen for many hours,
            And no one knows about his way or path.
            Hath he lost all his faithful, droidly sense?   125
            Most happ'ly would I by him be annoy'd,
            If it did mean that he, at least, were near.
HAN   I shall inquire of Lando 'bout the droid.

	But in the meantime, Leia, have no fear.	
LEIA	I trust not Lando.	
HAN	—Neither, sweet, do I,	130

But in the meantime, Leia, have no fear.

LEIA I trust not Lando.

HAN   —Neither, sweet, do I, 130
Yet he's my friend who helpeth us, dost see?
I'll warrant that we soon from here shall fly.

LEIA Then thou shalt take thy flight as well—from me.

HAN The future has its own time yet to write,
And wheth'r or not we worry, my good lass, 135
It comes as sure as day doth follow night.
So, think not of it till it come to pass.
     [Exeunt Han Solo and Princess Leia.

Enter a merry band of UGNAUGHTS,
singing as they pass around parts of C-3PO's body.

UGN. 1 O pass me that!

UGN. 2 O give me this!

UGN. 3 We Ugnaughts are a'working! 140

UGN. 2 O pass the head!

UGN. 3 Give me the chest!

UGN. 1 Our duties never shirking!

UGN. 3 Thou naughty droid—

UGN. 1 Thou hast been caught! 145

UGN. 2 Thy prying never ceases!

UGN. 1 Your lesson learn'd—

UGN. 2 Our treasures earn'd—

UGN. 3 For now thou art in pieces!

Enter CHEWBACCA.

CHEWBAC. Auugh! 150

[Chewbacca begins collecting pieces of C-3PO.

UGN. 2   Take not the arms!

UGN. 3   Pray, leave the legs!

UGN. 1   Thy greed thou art revealing!

UGN. 3   But naught shall last!

UGN. 1   For nothing doth!   155

UGN. 2   Our treasures thou art stealing!

UGN. 1   So shall we speak—

UGN. 2   Our proverb true—

UGN. 3   With voices loudly ringing—

UGN. 2   It easy came—   160

UGN. 3   And easy goes—

UGN. 1   But still we keep on singing!

[Exeunt Ugnaughts, singing.

Enter HAN SOLO *and* PRINCESS LEIA.

LEIA   I see, Chewbacca, thou hast found the droid,
            At least some small and varied parts of him.
            O, what hath happen'd?

CHEWBAC.   —Auugh!

HAN   —Thou hast found him   165
            Upon a junk pile, what? How can that be?
            C-3PO was fine when we arriv'd.
            But now, I fear, he is more dread than droid.

LEIA   'Tis such a mess. Canst thou repair him, good
            Chewbacca?

CHEWBAC.   —Egh, auugh.

HAN   —Lando's people can   170
            Provide the cure.

LEIA   —Nay, thank you: I'd not hav't.

Enter LANDO.

LANDO   Forgive me, worthy guests. Do I intrude?

LEIA   Nay, verily.

LANDO   —O, but thou art a beauty.
I prithee, never leave—thou dost belong
With us in our great city in the clouds.   175
Thy loveliness doth put the sun to shame,
Thy brightness of your cheek would shame the stars.

LEIA   [*aside:*] This scoundrel too familiar is. Now do
I see that though I once thought Han uncouth,
He is the sweetest smuggler ever liv'd.   180
[*To Lando:*] Thou hast my thanks.

LANDO   —Now come, will ye join me
For some repast?

CHEWBAC.   —Auugh.

LANDO   —Chewie, fear thou not!
Be sure I meant that all invited are.
[*Seeing C-3PO:*] Is there some matter with your droid?

HAN   —Nay, I
Know not of any matter.
         [*They walk, leaving C-3PO's parts.*
        Tell me, though,   185
As we proceed to supper: art thou an
Accepted member of the mining guild?

LANDO   Nay, we are none. Our operation is
Still small enough that we may be discreet.
'Tis advantageous to our customers,   190
For they are anxious to escape attention.

LEIA   [*aside:*] O, all this talk of bus'ness, mines and stealth!

My mind cannot abide it, for I sense
That terrible events shall soon befall.
Within my mind a vision of some pain   195
Begins to form, but still is indistinct.
Would that I had some time to clear my thoughts!

HAN   [*to Lando:*] But art thou not afraid the Empire shall
           Find out about your operation and
           Then drive you out of business, or e'en worse?   200

LANDO   'Tis e'er a danger that looms over us
           And all that we have built in Bespin's walls.
           But things have just develop'd which shall make
           Our future safe and well-secur'd. A deal
           I've with the Empire made that shall keep them   205
           Far distant from our operations.

                            [*They arrive at a door and open it.*

Enter DARTH VADER *and* BOBA FETT, *revealed inside.*

CHEWBAC.   —Auugh!

HAN   [*aside:*] But what is this? Betrayal! Hands, take flight—
           My blaster shall I use, and save us yet!

                            [*Han fires, but Vader deflects the blast
                            and uses the Force to takes Han's blaster.*

VADER   We would be honor'd should ye join us here.

LANDO   I am most sorry, worthy friend. They did   210
           Arrive in Bespin ere thou here didst fly.

HAN   No sorrier, I do expect, than I.

                                              [*Exeunt.*

SCENE 4.

Bespin, the cloud city.

Enter GUARDS 1 *and* 2.

GUARD 1   Oi! Well met, worthy friend. What dost thou here?
GUARD 2   I have been poring o'er our city's plans.
GUARD 1   What's this? A newfound interest? Shalt thou
    Turn architect?
GUARD 2   —Nay, nay, and yet I have
    Found something curious.
GUARD 1   —Indeed?
GUARD 2   —Indeed.   5
GUARD 1   Pray tell!
GUARD 2   —The city hath been built within
    The Empire's strict specifications for
    Design and building standards.
GUARD 1   —Aye, 'twas wise,
    Thus may the Bespin council never have
    A reason for to fear the Empire's sharp   10
    Inspectors.
GUARD 2   —Verily, but follow on:
    That they unto the code this city built
    Is not the thing that I found strange. Instead,
    It was the code's requirements I did mark.
    For didst thou know the Empire doth require   15
    That any major structure shall include
    At least one chasm that's deep and long and dark?
    Not only shall these chasms exist: the code
    Doth further specify that they shall be
    Abutting pathways where pedestrians   20

May walk. The Death Star that was built some years
Ago had, evidently, sev'ral of
These holes, and our Cloud City has them, too.
Is not this strange?

GUARD 1   —I know them well, and did
Go walking past just such a gaping hole   25
That led to nothingness but yesterday.
But wherefore dost thou say 'tis strange, I pray?

GUARD 2   It simply maketh little sense to put
Such vast, deep holes in ev'ry structure next
To well-worn paths. Could not a person, by   30
Some simple misstep, fall most easily
Down one of these great chasms? So wherefore place
Such hazards into ev'ry structure built?

GUARD 1   I see your reasoning, but shall rebut:
The Empire is the greatest strength e'er known,   35
    'Tis true?

GUARD 2   —Of course. I'd not say otherwise.

GUARD 1   And any great thing—person, beast, or realm—
Doth put its greatness on display, agreed?

GUARD 2   'Tis natural, I'll warrant. Pray, say on.

GUARD 1   I posit that the Empire doth command   40
That structures have these chasms immense because
It is through their immensity that our
Great Empire's strength is shown. And since they are
Vast holes that deadly are, should one fall in,
They send a message strong and clear to all: 45
The Empire is a proud and mighty pow'r
And doth not fear sure death, but laughs at it.
I' faith, we are so full of life that we
Walk by our certain passing daily—it

Is but quotidian for us—and yet   50
We have no fear.

GUARD 2   —Thy point is clearly made.
But still, I think it strange that this is true:
A structure is not whole till it hath holes.
Such things lie far beyond my understanding,
Yet do I trust there is a master plan.   55

GUARD 1   Shall we to supper, friend?

GUARD 2   —Forsooth, lead on!

                    [*Exeunt Guards 1 and 2.*

                    Enter LANDO.

LANDO   O what is this dire sound I just have heard?
My friend Han Solo screaming in great pain,
The shrieks of man turn'd victim through my fault—
My quick decision to protect myself.   60
Yet what choice had I? Could I else have done?
No person in my place would diff'rently
Behave. No choice had I but one: to save
Myself, my interests, and my belov'd
Cloud City from a dark and awful fate.   65
Yet ever shall my soul be haunted by
These dismal howls of my old friend, unless
I can find some way to make recompense.
But how shall that e'er be whilst Vader's threats
Do cast their shadows o'er my ev'ry move?   70
I know not how, but yet it must be so.
I shall—belike with loyal Lobot's help—
Discover yet a way to make this right,
And save myself from a betrayer's name!

Enter LOBOT, DARTH VADER, *and* BOBA FETT.

VADER   [*to Boba Fett:*] Thou mayst take Captain Solo
                               and transport   75
    Him unto Jabba once Skywalker has
    Arriv'd and captur'd been. Say, is this clear?

FETT   'Tis, my Lord. But Solo is no good to me, should
    he be dead upon delivery. He hath been tortur'd
    severely in this last hour. 'Tis well, but I prithee do   80
    not kill the man ere I deliver him to Jabba.

VADER   No harm beyond undoing shall he bear.

LANDO   Lord Vader, do I comprehend this fully—
    Thou shalt surrender Han unto this man,
    This bounty hunter here? So what is next?   85
    I prithee, tell me: what shall happen to
    Both Leia and the Wookiee?

VADER   —Never shall
    They leave this city.

LANDO   —This doth push the bounds
    Too far! Imprisonment was never a
    Condition of the bargain we did make,   90
    And 'twas not in the plan to hand o'er Han
    Unto this bounty hunter!

VADER   —Mayhap thou
    Dost think thou hast unfairly treated been?

LANDO   [*aside:*] A threat is in his voice and aspect. [*To Vader:*]
                                      Nay,
    For I shall model flexibility.   95

VADER   'Tis well. 'Twould be a pity should I feel
    It necessary to retain a full
    And armor'd garrison in Bespin. [*To Boba Fett:*] Come!

                                    [Exeunt Darth Vader and Boba Fett.
LANDO   He orders what he will sans sense or rhyme—
               This deal is worse becoming all the time!   100
LOBOT   . . .

                                                    [Exeunt.

SCENE 5.

Bespin, the cloud city.

Enter CHEWBACCA, *with* C-3PO's *parts.*

CHEWBAC. Auugh.

C-3PO [*being reconnected:*] —Stormtroopers? In Bespin?
                                              I am shot!
                    [*Chewbacca disconnects C-3PO and
                           tries to reconnect him again.*

CHEWBAC. Egh!

C-3PO   —O, 'tis better! That is quite improv'd.
          But hold, for something is not right: my eyes—
          I cannot see.
                              [*Chewbacca adjusts C-3PO.*
                    Now that is mended, aye.
          Yet wait, I now am backward—head is back   5
          And front's reverse and all has gone awry!
          Is this a Wookiee's notion of a joke?
          Thou stupid, senseless beast!

CHEWBAC. [*laughing:*]   —Gihut, gihut!

C-3PO Thou furball wretched! Mophead ignorant!
                    [*Chewbacca switches off C-3PO.*

Enter HAN SOLO, *carried by* STORMTROOPERS,
          who drop him and exit.

CHEWBAC. Auugh, auugh!

HAN   —O, Chewie, I'm in agony—   10
          My ev'ry bone and sinew cries with pain.

Enter Princess Leia.

LEIA   What have they done to you, my noble man?
              And what can be their purpose, dost thou know?
HAN   'Twas torture unlike any I have known,
              For never any questions did they ask.   15
              Instead, with silent mouths and darting eyes
              They fix'd me solidly unto a seat
              And lower'd me unto a mechanism.
              At first 'twas like a searing heat that rac'd
              From skin to bone and back again. Then sparks   20
              Flew out, upon my chest and neck and face,
              Such fire as though a hundred blasters spread
              Their shots across my body or, perhaps,
              As though a million tiny lightsabers
              Did prick and dance their way about my skin.   25
              All this they did, but ne'er made inquiry,
              Ne'er ask'd me whence we came or where we go,
              Ne'er ask'd about the rebels' rendezvous.
              No information they did seek to know,
              It only seem'd they wish'd to bring me pain.   30
              I tell thee, 'twas far worse and terrible
              Than if they had sought answers from my blood.
              But this demented evil shakes my soul,
              For wherefore torture without questioning?

Enter Lando, *with* GUARDS.

CHEWBAC. Auugh, egh, auugh!
HAN   —Get thee hence now, Lando.
LANDO   —Tut!   35

Attend my voice, for this ye both should hear:
Darth Vader hath giv'n word that he will turn
Both Leia and Chewbacca o'er to me.

HAN   What dost thou mean by "o'er to me"? Thou knave!
             I would not turn a rival o'er to thee,   40
             Much less the ones belovèd by my heart.

LANDO   They must stay here, but will, at least, be safe.
             'Twas not my choice—I have no say in this.
             'Tis Vader who doth pull the strings, and we
             Are but the puppets with which he doth play.   45

LEIA   And what of Han?

LANDO   —Darth Vader shall give him
             O'er to the bounty hunter.

LEIA   —Vader doth
             Desire that all of us are dead.

LANDO   —He wants
             You not at all. He searches for someone
             Called Skywalker.

HAN   —Aye, Luke—thou meanest Luke!   50

LANDO   Lord Vader set a trap for him to fall.

LEIA   And we are but the bait by which he's caught.

LANDO   The trap shall soon be sprung, for Skywalker
             Is on his way, e'en now.

HAN   —This villainy
             Thou hast arrang'd is all too perfect. Fie!   55

                         [Han Solo strikes Lando but is
                              quickly restrained by guards.

CHEWBAC.   Auugh!

LANDO   —Cease! I have done all that I may do.
             For certain I am sorry I could not
             Do better yet than this, but I do have

Enough vexations here.

HAN   —O, thou great man!
Thou art a hero, and thy tale shall e'er   60
Upon the lips of lesser folk be told.
Throughout all history it shall be writ:
"Behold, great Lando of Calrissian,
A man who ever serv'd his comrades well."

LANDO   [*aside:*] This stings my soul, yet no more can I do   65
Than hold my head up high, and plan what's next.

[Exeunt Lando and guards.

LEIA   My soldier, O my heart, thy fire doth blaze!
Thy skill with others ne'er doth cease t'amaze.

[Exeunt.

ACT V

SCENE 1.

Bespin, the cloud city.

Enter UGNAUGHTS 1, 2, *and* 3, *singing.*

UGN. 3	The time is ripe!	
UGN. 1	His time is nigh!	
UGN. 2	And soon he will be frozen!	
UGN. 1	We've never done—	
UGN. 2	This on a man—	5
UGN. 3	But someone's now been chosen!	
UGN. 2	A merry prank!	
UGN. 3	O shall it work?	
UGN. 1	Or will the man be dying?	
UGN. 3	What'er befall—	10
UGN. 1	One thing is sure—	
UGN. 2	The pleasure's in the trying!	

[Exeunt Ugnaughts.

Enter LANDO, LOBOT, DARTH VADER, *and* BOBA FETT.

VADER   A perfect touch this is, to freeze Skywalker.
          The plan is perfect—he who hath destroy'd
          The Death Star shall be packag'd as a gift.   15
          But now, let us inspect the details. Aye,
          This crude contraption should be adequate
          To put this vexing Skywalker on ice
          Ere his deliv'ry to the Emperor.

Enter IMPERIAL SOLDIER.

SOLDIER   Lord Vader—there's a ship that doth approach,   20
            An X-wing class.
VADER   —'Tis well. Watch Skywalker,
            Allow his landing, let him hither come.
                                          [*Exit Imperial soldier.*
LANDO   Lord Vader, this facility has ne'er
            Been us'd for humans, only carbon freezing.
            If thou dost put him in this vast machine   25
            It may not freeze him, but may mean his death.
VADER   This is a point that I consider'd not.
            It seems, Calrissian, that thou dost learn
            To be obedient unto thy Lord.
            'Tis well, and it is in thine interest.   30
            I do not wish him harm'd; the Emperor
            Shall not enjoy a damag'd prize. So shall
            Another stand for him to be a test—
            We shall make Captain Solo undergo
            The freezing process first, to test its pow'r.   35
FETT   My Lord, although his death would bring me
            joy, it doth not pay. Jabba, like thine Emperor,
            giveth no fees for damag'd goods. I prithee,
            what shall happen if the man doth die? What
            then, for Boba Fett?   40
VADER   Fear not, thy hunt shall have its bounty still.
            Thou shalt be compensated if he dies.

            Enter HAN SOLO, CHEWBACCA, PRINCESS LEIA, *and*
            C-3PO *(attached to Chewbacca's back), all guarded.*

C-3PO   [*to Chewbacca:*] I almost fully am restor'd to my
            Old self, except thy work is not complete.

	If thou had but attach'd my legs, I would	45
	Not yet remain in this position rare!	
	I prithee, good Chewbacca, do recall	
	That I am thy responsibility—	
	Do not in any instance foolish be!	

HAN   [*to Lando:*] Pray tell, O dearest friend, what is at hand? 50

LANDO   Thou shalt be plac'd in total carbon freeze.

HAN   [*aside:*] The news of my grim fate doth chill my blood.

O, how I once thought Hoth was cold and bleak,

Yet now I pine for all its balmy plains.

VADER   Now, put him in!

CHEWBAC.   —Auugh!

[Chewbacca fights guards and
slays three of them.

HAN   —Chewie, stop, I pray!   55

C-3PO   Alas, yes, stop! I am not set to die!

HAN   This cannot help me, brave Chewbacca, nay.

I prithee, save thy strength to fight again.

Attend me now: the princess—thou must be

Her strength, her stay, her guard, her confidence: 60

These things that I no longer can bestow.

LEIA   O, I do love thee wholly, Han.

HAN   —I know.

[Han is placed into the machine and
emerges in a frozen block.

C-3PO   Pray, turn around, Chewbacca, let me see.

O, he in carbonite hath been encas'd—

He should be well protected, if he hath   65

Surviv'd the freezing process.

VADER   —Make report,

Calrissian, is he alive?

LANDO	—He is,
	And rests in perfect hibernation here.
VADER	The prize is thine now, bounty hunter Fett.
	Take him to Jabba, with my gratitude. 70
FETT	[*aside:*] Aye, prize, indeed, and worthy of
	the wait. To Tatooine I fly, with expectation
	of payment great.
VADER	Reset the chamber for young Skywalker—
	He shall the next a'freezing undergo. 75

Enter IMPERIAL SOLDIER.

SOLDIER	Skywalker's ship hath just made landing, Lord.
VADER	'Tis well, and be thou sure he hither comes—
	Put him upon the path that leads him here.
	[Exit Imperial soldier.
	Calrissian, take thou the princess and
	The Wookiee to my ship, and there remain. 80
LANDO	Nay, thou didst say they would in Bespin dwell—
	With me, under my supervision keen.
	How canst thou bargain thus? 'Tis always thy
	Side of the deal that doth improve. What shalt
	Thou give to me to make this deal worthwhile? 85
VADER	Seek not to deal thyself a winning hand.
	The Empire shall not e'er play by thy rules.
	By my command, the deal is alterèd.
	In all thy orisons thou mayst yet plead
	The deal no further alterèd will be. 90
	[Exeunt Darth Vader and Boba Fett. Chewbacca
	and Princess Leia sing a song of lament.
CHEWBAC.	[*sings:*] Auugh, egh, auugh, auugh egh. Auugh,

                                                   muh, muh,

             Egh, egh, auugh, egh, egh, muh, muh.

             Auugh, auugh, egh, auugh, muh, egh, muh, muh,

             Muh, wroshyr, wroshyr, wroshyr.

LEIA   [*sings:*] Full fathom five my lover lies,   95

             Within an icy tomb,

             They say he lives, yet my heart dies,

             Sing wroshyr, wroshyr, wroshyr.

CHEWBAC.   [*sings:*] Egh, auugh, auugh, auugh, egh, egh,

                                      muh, muh,

             Auugh, egh, egh, auugh, auugh, muh, muh.   100

             Egh, auugh, auugh, grrm, auugh, egh, muh, muh,

             Muh, wroshyr, wroshyr, wroshyr.

LEIA   [*sings:*] Now he is gone, and so's my life,

             All frozen in a moment.

             He my seiz'd lov'd one, I his strife,   105

             Sing wroshyr, wroshyr, wroshyr.

                                    [Exeunt.

SCENE 2.

Bespin, the cloud city.

Enter LUKE SKYWALKER, *with* R2-D2 *behind.*

LUKE   Yes, now am I in Bespin—more fool I,

             For though my feelings say this is the place,

             I know not yet for certain if it be.

             My friends I have not heard from, hide nor hair,

             And yet the Force doth call in clearest tones   5

             As if to say: "Here lies thy destiny!"

                 [Luke sees Bespin guards carrying Han Solo.
But wait, what's this? Procession most sincere,
And with such maimèd rites? This doth betoken
The corpse they follow was an enemy.
These Bespin guards do make odd pallbearers;   10
This scene is verily a sign of ill.

     Enter BOBA FETT, *shooting at Luke. Luke shoots back.*
                Exit Boba Fett.

Aha! It seems that I expected am—
This then must be the place my vision saw.
The Force hath led me here by prophet's hand—
I shall pursue the fiend most ardently,   15
Belike he shall lead me unto my mates.
               [Exeunt Luke and R2-D2.

     Enter CHEWBACCA, PRINCESS LEIA, *and* LANDO,
        with GUARDS *and* BOBA FETT.

LANDO   These blasts and great commotion indicate
          Skywalker's recent advent unto Bespin.
          This great upheaval his arrival makes
          Doth grant me the diversion that I seek   20
          To call upon my man-at-arms for help.
               [Lando presses buttons on
                    his wrist communicator.

     Enter LUKE SKYWALKER *and* R2-D2.
        Boba Fett shoots again.

LEIA   O Luke, pray fly! 'Tis but a trap! A trap!
          Flee now, dear friend, ere thou art captur'd too.
LUKE   But what is this? 'Tis Leia in distress!
          Yet here, beset by blasts, I'll not prevail.   25
                    [Exit Luke Skywalker under fire, with R2-D2
                                    behind him. Exit Boba Fett.

          Enter LOBOT *with* ARMED BATTALION.

CHEWBAC. Auugh!
LANDO   —Aye, well done, my aide! Pray, put them in
          The tower most secure, and be ye quiet!
LOBOT   . . .
                    [Exeunt Lobot with battalion and Imperial guards.
LEIA   [*aside:*] O, will he play the hero now? A fig!
          [*To Lando:*] What is in thy imagination, man?   30
LANDO   We shall depart at once.
                    [He releases the bands from Chewbacca's hands.
C-3PO   [*aside:*]   —I knew 'twas thus,
          A regular misunderstanding.
                            [Chewbacca begins to choke Lando.
CHEWBAC.   —Auugh!
LANDO   [*choking:*] I had no choice!
C-3PO   —What is this foolishness?
          Pray, trust him!
LEIA   —Aye, we understand, thou knave,
          Thou didst have neither choice nor will to act.   35
          Thou brute! Imperi'l officers act by
          Their Lord's command and blind obedience,
          The bounty hunter is well paid for his
          Nefari'us actions, e'en Darth Vader and

The Emperor are fully driven by   40
Their power, aye! But shalt thou say thou hadst
No choice? What lily-liver'd weak excuse
Is this? At least assume thy stature as
A man, and here confess thy shameful deeds!
We'll give thee opportunity to 'fess   45
Thy wrongs before thou diest at Chewie's hand.

LANDO   [*choking:*] I did but try to help.

LEIA   —We do not need
Thy help, thou whoreson, senseless villain!

LANDO   [*choking:*]   —Han!

LEIA   What didst thou say?

C-3PO   —It sounded like a "Han!"

LANDO   [*choking:*] There may yet be a chance we can save

                                              Han.   50
The bounty hunter's ship, the platform east.

LEIA   Pray, Chewie, let him go.
          [*Chewbacca releases Lando. He and Princess Leia*
                    begin to walk away, followed by Lando.

C-3PO   —My ferventest
Apologies for this, good Sir. See, he
Is but a Wookiee, ignorant and plain.

          Enter BOBA FETT *on balcony, with* GUARDS
              and the frozen body of HAN SOLO.

FETT   Now put him in the cargo hold. Who now   55
hath been victorious, Solo? Who is the winner
clear? And as the victor, so go the spoils. Jabba's
bounty and his great pleasure shall I enjoy when
I arrive with thee on Tatooine. I shall become a

courtier in the palace of the Hutts ere this is   60
through. Boba Fett triumphant!

                [Exeunt Boba Fett and guards.

                Enter R2-D2.

R2-D2   [*aside:*] I have been separated from my master.
                Yet happy circumstance, for here I see
                The others, and may now rejoin them.
                            [*To C-3PO:*] Squeak!

C-3PO   O R2, R2, say, where hast thou been?   65
                It does me well to see thee, little droid.
                Yet prithee, haste thee, for we all now strive
                To save our captain from the clutches of
                The bounty hunter!

R2-D2   —Meep, beep, whistle, squeak!

C-3PO   At least thou art still in one piece—observe   70
                My sad fragmented fate!

                    [They arrive at the east platform to
                        see Boba Fett's ship flying away.

LEIA   [*aside:*]   —O flown, alack!
                My Han—his body flown and fled. Now break
                My heart, and weep mine eyes. A princess I
                May be, but first and foremost human with
                Emotions that betray my higher sense.   75
                O gracious Han, forgive that I did come
                To love thee late, and only then to lose thee.
                I'll find thee in the stars, my Han—I'll search
                The galaxy until I find thee.

C-3PO   —O!
                [*To Chewbacca:*] Pray, Chewie, look, they come
                                  behind thee!

CHEWBAC.   —Egh!   80

Enter STORMTROOPERS *from behind, who battle with*
CHEWBACCA, PRINCESS LEIA, *and* LANDO.
The stormtroopers are slain.

LEIA   The soldiers are dispatch'd; now let us go.
              A princess doth command thee, Lando: make
              Thy choice once and for all whom thou shalt serve.
              Wilt thou remain the Empire's stooge, or shalt
              Thou go with us to serve rebellion's cause?   85
LANDO   Good lady, this demand is fairly made.
              Forgive me of the things I've done, I pray,
              And I shall fly with thee and serve thee true.
              But first, let me a final action take
              To serve the Bespinites I love so well—   90
              One moment for the greater good. [*Into comlink:*]
                                          Hear ye,
              'Tis Lando of Calrissian who speaks.
              The Empire doth control the city now—
              I do advise ye all: evacuate
              At once, before more troops arrive within.   95
                        [*Lando tries to open a door and fails.*
              [*To Princess Leia:*] This door shall lead us to the
                                          Falcon, but
              The codes have chang'd. I know not how!
C-3PO   —R2,
              Thou canst o'erride the door's security.
              Pray, R2, speed thee!
                        [*R2-D2 tries to plug into the computer
                                          and gets shocked.*

R2-D2   —Beep, meep, whistle, beep!

C-3PO   O blame me not, I am interpreter,   100
And know not power socket from computer!
[More stormtroopers enter and begin to
shoot at Chewbacca, Princess Leia, and Lando.

LANDO   Now under siege again! O, let us hence
Away unto the *Falcon.* Droid, canst thou
Release these doors that we may pass and fly?

LEIA   If ever droid were worthy, R2 is.   105
Go to it, R2, make our good escape!

R2-D2   Beep, meep, beep, beep, squeak, whistle, beep, meep,
meep!

C-3PO   We do not care about the hyperdrive—
The great *Millenn'um Falcon* is repair'd!

R2-D2   [*aside:*] Fie! This computer tells me all's not well,   110
But how shall I convey this 'midst these blasts?
The doorway first; the hyperdrive shall wait.
[*To C-3PO:*] Beep, meep!

C-3PO   —Pray, ope' the door, thou stupid lump!
[The door opens.
O, R2, never did I doubt thee, thou
Art wonderful!
[Exeunt R2-D2, Lando, and Chewbacca
with C-3PO, into the Millennium Falcon.

LEIA   —I know that I should fly,   115
And yet for Han's sake would I stay and slay
Each enemy that cometh from within.
Love unfulfill'd turns quickly into spite,
And vengefulness doth fill the empty place
Within my heart. O die a thousand times,   120
Ye basest beasts who fed upon my love.

O brutes, ye think not of the lives ye take—
You are but senseless minions who fulfill
The sordid whims of your Imperi'l lords.
Belike 'tis not your fault, for you are by   125
A merciless, vile Emperor controll'd.
Yet I shall strike at ye till you do fall
For ev'ry pain that you have giv'n to me:
The loss of Alderaan, of my great friends,
And now the loss of my belovèd one.   130
O die, ye mindless men of Empire cruel!
I shall upon the Empire be reveng'd
Until my gallant Han hath been aveng'd.

> [Exit Princess Leia.

SCENE 3.

Bespin, the cloud city.

Enter LUKE SKYWALKER.

LUKE   Where am I now, and where are all my friends?
Some wrong turn have I ta'en, and now am lost
Within a cavern, dark and fill'd with mist.
R2 is left behind; I am alone.
What evil lurks within this passage bleak?   5
What fate shall I discover in this place?
What pow'r hath brought me here—is it the Force?
If not, what messenger of darkness vile
Hath giv'n me up unto this realm of fear?
The cold I feel is as on Dagobah,   10
When in the cave my darkest self I fac'd.

The thoughts I thought therein do now return,
The questions that did rise and give me pause:
O, what is life, and what our purpose here?
Are living creatures made for pain and strife,   15
Do we but walk our days upon the ground
To perish without memory or fame?
If so, what shall we seek whilst we yet live?
Is brave adventure worthy of our time,
Or should we seek the principle of pleasure?   20
Are family and children noble aims,
Or is the Force itself our holy goal?
Is life a quest or is it but a farce—
A splendid journey or a fool's crusade?
Such questions plague my soul, and make me doubt.   25
They draw my mind toward the darkest thoughts
That e'er I've known since I became a man.
And here, away from Dagobah, I have
No firm assurance of my safety, nor
The comfort of my master being here.   30
Thus shall I face my fortune by myself,
Without my mentors great to give me help.
The thought doth bring me trepidation, for
I have relie'd upon their counsel wise.
Be with me here in spirit, if not form,   35
Good Obi-Wan and Yoda—masters true.
O life, O Fate! I would I knew my place,
My time, my end, my destiny complete—
But I cannot see why or how life is.
Because the past is not a perfect guide,   40
And since the future still remains unknown:
My fate shall I meet in the present tense.

                                                 [A sound is heard.
        But soft, I hear slow footsteps drawing near.

                  Enter DARTH VADER.

VADER	The Force is with thee now, young Skywalker,	
	In troth—but thou art not a Jedi yet.	45
LUKE	[*aside:*] 'Tis Vader, and 'tis Fate. Let it begin.	

                                         [They duel.

                  Enter CHORUS.

CHORUS	O mighty duel, O action ne'er surpass'd:	
	The lightsabers do clash and glow like fire.	
	Darth Vader in the villain's role is cast,	
	While Luke's young temper turneth soon to ire.	50
	They flash and fly like dancers in a set,	
	Yet never dance did know such deadly mood.	
	Luke tires, and soon his brow begins to sweat,	
	Whilst Vader doth attack with strength renew'd.	
VADER	Forsooth, young one, 'tis plain thou hast learn'd much.	55
LUKE	Thou shalt find me full of surprises yet!	
VADER	Thy destiny doth lie with me, Skywalker.	
	Your teacher Obi-Wan did know 'twas true.	
LUKE	Thou liest, O thou villain cruel and cold.	

                    [They duel, and Luke falls into the carbon
                                    freezing machine.

VADER	[*aside:*] 'Twas far too simple, trapping him within.	60
	Perhaps the boy is not as powerful	
	As my great Emperor and I did think.	

                  [Luke leaps out of the carbon freezing machine.

LUKE   I am not captur'd yet, thou lord of hate.
              Thou must another evil scheme derive
              To catch me in thy snares. For I am quick,   65
              And move with all the power of the Force.

VADER   Impressive, most impressive, worthy lad,
              Thine Obi-Wan hath taught thee well, and thou
              Hast master'd all thy fears. Now, go! Release
              Thine anger, for thy hate alone can strike   70
              Me down! [*Aside:*] Now 'tis the moment to provoke
              His inner rage. Come walls, machines, and parts
              And come at him from ev'ry side. He'll be
              Made weak, and in his weakness darkness find!

                         [*Darth Vader uses the Force to strike*
                              Luke with nearby objects.

LUKE   Alas, I fall—O Fate, be on my side!   75

                              [*Luke falls out a window.*

VADER   The battle goes exactly as foreseen.
              The boy is powerful and skill'd, 'tis true,
              But his young powers are no match for mine.
              It seems that Obi-Wan was weak with age,
              For this boy's training still is incomplete.   80
              He shall be turnèd yet, for I still hold
              The news that shall undo him utterly.
              He thinks the speed of my lightsaber and
              My power to send objects hurtling at
              Him are the worst that I can muster, but   85
              My greatest weapon yet shall break his soul,
              Not touch his body. He shall know the truth.
              But even as I plan to share with him
              The story of his father, I must pause.
              The strange confusion I before have felt   90

Hath come again into my mind. What is't?
I know no better Fate for him and me
Than to be join'd in service to my Lord
And Emperor. So why am I confus'd?
Enough of this now, Vader: finish it.   95
The boy shall turn or he shall be destroy'd.

> *[Exit Darth Vader. Luke begins to*
> *climb through the window.*

LUKE   O pain, O bitter weariness. I did
Not know the power of the Force till now—
Till it, to purpose rank, was turn'd on me!
Now for my very life I grasp and hold   100
Unto the precipice whereon I cling.
Be with me now, O Ben, restore my strength.
I see that Vader hath ta'en flight, yet it
Is plain he doth but wait for his next chance.
Some hope remains, e'en now, amidst my fear—   105
He may yet be defeated, all's not lost.
I have regain'd my footing, and may rest
Until the fight must be resum'd. Now quick:
Look deep within your heart, Luke, and recall
The teachings of your gentle master Yoda.   110
Breathe deeply and call on the Force, that it
May show to thee the path that thou must take.
O, give me strength to win this battle now
Or, if not win, maintain my sense of right.
But lo, Darth Vader cometh once again!   115

Enter DARTH VADER. *They duel, and Luke*
is forced to the edge of a deep cavern.

VADER This is the end for thee, Skywalker. See,
       Thou art defeated now; resistance would
       Be futile. Let yourself not be destroy'd
       As Obi-Wan did, weak old man he was.
                       [They duel. Darth Vader cuts off Luke's
                            right hand with his lightsaber.
LUKE   O horror! O vast pain exceeding words!   120
VADER Thou shalt find no escape. Do not make me
       Destroy thee. Great importance shalt thou have
       Within the Empire's power, and thine own
       Shall only grow with time. I prithee, join
       With me, and I your training shall complete.   125
       When our strength is combin'd, we shall conclude
       This bitter conflict and bring order to
       The galaxy entire.
LUKE   —I never shall
       Join with thee; I would rather be destroy'd.
VADER [aside:] The boy doth admirably keep his head,   130
       But now I shall unleash the final blow.
       [To Luke:] If thou but knewest all the power of
       The dark side. Obi-Wan hath never told
       Thee of what happen'd to thy father, Luke.
LUKE   O, he hath spoken much. And he hath told   135
       Me of the truth—that thou didst slay him, aye,
       And without cause or mercy, murderer
       Most vile and wretched!
VADER   —No, I am thy father.
LUKE   Nay, 'tis not true! It is impossible!
VADER Pray, search thy feelings, Luke. Thou knowest it   140
       Is true.
LUKE   —Nay!

VADER   —Luke, thou mayst the Emperor
            Destroy; he hath foreseen what thou wouldst do.
            It is thy destiny, come join with me—
            Together we shall rule the galaxy
            As son and father. Come now, Luke, it is   145
            The only way: the dark side is thy path.
            O join with me, and we shall be as one.
                    [Luke looks down and drops into the cavern.

LUKE   I fall, and yet no death's upon me yet.
            I fall, for 'tis a better path than hate.

VADER   He falls, and welcomes death instead of pow'r.   150
            He falls, but I can sense he liveth still.

LUKE   I have not died—but pass into this shaft.
            I have not died—though I may wish it so.

VADER   He hath not died—his heart screams in its fear.
            He hath not died—so may he yet be turn'd.   155
                        [Luke falls onto a weather vane at
                                the bottom of the shaft.

LUKE   I am held fast by this vane o'er the clouds.
            I am held fast by some mirac'lous pow'r.

VADER   He is held fast within the dark side's grasp.
            He is held fast by his own clouded mind.
                                    [Exit Darth Vader.

LUKE   O Ben, I call to thee, but wilt thou hear?   160
            I do remember thou didst say thou couldst
            Not interfere in this, but O Ben, hear!
            Alas, my mentor's gone fore'er, and gives
            No answer—e'en deserted by the dead.
            If he cannot appear and rescue me,   165
            Then I shall try the living: Leia, next
            I call to thee. I prithee, Leia, hear!

Enter CHEWBACCA, PRINCESS LEIA, *and* LANDO,
aside in the Millennium Falcon.

LEIA   [*aside:*] What is this voice that echoes in mine ears?
          'Tis Luke, I know it is. Yet how is it
          That I do hear him when he is not nigh?   170
          No matter—more important 'tis that I
          Respond unto his call. [*To Lando:*] We must go back.
LANDO   What didst thou say?
LEIA   —I know where Luke is!
LANDO   —What
          About the fighters drawing near?
CHEWBAC.   —Egh, auugh!
LEIA   I prithee, Chewie: Han we could not save,   175
          But may yet rescue Luke, if we make haste.
LANDO   But what about the fighters, Princess?
CHEWBAC.   —Auugh!
LANDO   Pray, peace, good Wookiee, thou shalt have thy way.
                 [They approach Luke in the ship. Lando
                 breaks off from the others to let Luke in.
          What ties most deep do bind these souls as one!
          In all my workings as a bus'nessman,   180
          In all my making deals and earning more,
          I have forgotten what doth make life rich:
          'Tis friendship, love, and sacrifice that make
          A life, and I too long have not liv'd well!
          Farewell, the former Lando, lonely man!   185
          Farewell to selfish pride and high ambition!
          Farewell to scoundrelhood and avarice!
          Farewell to all the things my life has been!
          From now, I shall the great Rebellion serve,

And join myself unto this band of friends   190
Whate'er befall—pain, injury, or death.

         [Lando opens the hatch.
         Luke drops from the weather vane
                 into the ship.

Now come, brave Luke, whose mates to thee are dear,
I have not met thee, but do call thee brother.
Give me your hand, good Sir, if we be friends,
And Lando shall, in time, restore amends.   195
[To Leia:] Good Princess, let us fly, for all is well!

LEIA   O Luke, my heart doth swell to see thee safe!
Thou hast been caught within Darth Vader's trap,
But now thou art deliver'd and restor'd.

         [Luke and Leia embrace while Lando
               returns to the cockpit.

Now go with me unto the cot, and rest.   200
In time, we shall trade tales of grief and woe.

LANDO   The man is sav'd, but now the battle's on,
For by TIE fighters is our ship pursu'd!

LEIA   The *Falcon* is attack'd, Luke. Lie thou back,
I shall anon return to give thee aid.   205

         [Leia goes to the cockpit.

[To Lando:] Behold, a Star Destroyer doth approach.

LANDO   Make ready, Chewie, for the lightspeed jump.

LEIA   Aye, if thy people fix'd the hyperdrive,
Coordinates are set—'tis time we flew.

LANDO   Now make it so!

         [The Millennium Falcon *makes a sound and fails.*

CHEWBAC.   —Auugh!

LANDO   —I was told 'twas fix'd!   210
My trust I gave them, to repair the ship.

Some treachery and villainy lie here.
Forgive me, I know not what hath transpir'd.
'Tis not my fault. In troth, 'tis not my fault!

Enter DARTH VADER *and* ADMIRAL PIETT *on balcony.*

PIETT   The ship shall be in tractor beaming range   215
             Before thou canst say "aye."
VADER   —Thy trusty men
             Disab'd the swift *Falcon*'s hyperdrive?
PIETT   They did, my Lord.
VADER   —'Tis well. Prepare to board
             Their ship, and set all weapons onto stun.
             They have not made escape for long, and soon   220
             Skywalker shall be in my hand again,
             And I shall bring him to the Emperor.
PIETT   Indeed, my Lord, I shall with joy comply.
             The rebels shall be in our grasp anon.
             [Exit Admiral Piett, while Darth Vader stares into space.

Enter C-3PO *and* R2-D2, *who is repairing* C-3PO.

C-3PO   Why have we not to lightspeed flown?
R2-D2   —Beep, squeak!   225
C-3PO   What dost thou mean that we cannot? How canst
             Thou know the hyperdrive disabl'd is?
R2-D2   Beep, meep, meep, beep, squeak, whistle, nee, beep,
                                                    hoo!
C-3PO   The city's central processor hath told
             Thee so? O, R2-D2, how have I   230
             Oft warnèd thee of talking to a strange

Computer? Now, attend to my repair!
                    [R2-D2 continues to repair C-3PO.

VADER   [*to Luke:*] Luke, well I know that thou canst sense
                                        my call.

LUKE   My father! Word most strange upon my lips.

VADER   My son.

LUKE   —O Ben, why didst thou tell me not?   235
                    [Luke walks to the cockpit.

LANDO   Chewbacca, we must fly or we shall be
Destroy'd!

LUKE   —It is Darth Vader on that ship.
We are in danger here. When shall we fly?

VADER   Luke, come with me, fulfill thy destiny!

LUKE   [*aside:*] O Ben, I ask, why didst thou tell me not?   240
What anguish and disorder fill my mind!
                    [R2-D2 goes to the control panel.

R2-D2   [*aside:*] It falls to me again to win the day,
And rescue the Rebellion from dire loss.
I shall reactivate the hyperdrive,
Thus we shall fly, to fight another time!   245

C-3PO   O clever droid, great R2, rescuer!
                    [R2-D2 adjusts the control panel and the
                    Millennium Falcon flies into lightspeed.
                    Exeunt all but Darth Vader.

VADER   Fie, fie! Yet once again the ship escapes.
I shall devise brave punishments for those
Who put upon our state this grievous blight.
Then shall I seek my son, the Jedi Knight.   250
                    [Exit Darth Vader.

SCENE 4.

Aboard a rebel cruiser.

Enter LUKE SKYWALKER.

LUKE   The medic droid hath fix'd my hand with care,
Though never shall it fully be repair'd.
For though I can this hand use as before,
It shall ne'er truly be a hand of mine.
For now I am machine, though partly so,   5
Now have I ta'en a step toward the man
Who saith he is my father, yet is wires
And bolts. O hand, I find thee yet so dear.
Pray, serve me well, and prick my memory
That I did once the dark side briefly know—   10
And fac'd, and fought, and ultimately fail'd.
Then rise once more with me, my true right hand—
Thy rightful place thou shalt take at my side
To right the wrongs that we have sufferèd,
And right now thou and I begin to work   15
T'ward righteousness in great rebellion's cause.

Enter CHEWBACCA, PRINCESS LEIA, *and* LANDO.

      Now Lando, shalt thou go?
LANDO   —Aye, Luke, for all
Hath been prepar'd. When we find Jabba and
The bounty hunter, we shall tell thee all.
LUKE   I'll meet thee where we plann'd—on Tatooine—   20
My homeland that is now estrang'd from me.
LANDO   Good princess, now farewell. Apologies

Most earnest I convey again, and with
Them come a vow: we shall find Han, I swear.

LUKE   Dear Chewie, I'll await thy signal.

CHEWBAC.   —Auugh!   25

LUKE   Now take thou care—the Force be with ye both.

[*They move to separate parts of the stage.*

LANDO   Now ends this troubl'd time of Empire's rise,
Our time of harsh betrayal, painful loss.
Now have we learn'd what friendship truly costs,
And in the learning lost a comrade strong.   30

LEIA   Along the way, our hearts were movèd much:
By sacred love, most wondrous to behold,
By bravery that shall outlive the times,
By sacrifice of our most precious friends.

LUKE   Encounters unexpected we did meet   35
With masters wise and persons unforeseen.
These are the star wars, yet they are not done—
For sure, the final chapter's just begun.

Enter CHORUS *as epilogue.*

CHORUS   A glooming peace this morning with it brings,
No shine of starry light or planet's glow.   40
For though our heroes 'scape the Empire's slings,
The great rebellion ne'er has been so low.
Brave Han is for the Empire's gain betray'd,
Which doth leave Princess Leia's heart full sore.
Young Luke hath had his hand repair'd, remade—   45
The man is whole, but shaken to the core.
Forgive us, gentles, for this brutal play,
This tale of sorrow, strife, and deepest woes.

Ye must leave empty, sighing lack-a-day,
Till we, by George, a brighter play compose.   50
Our story endeth, though your hearts do burn,
And shall until the Jedi doth return.

[Exeunt omnes.

END.

AFTERWORD.

A Winter's Tale, indeed: *William Shakespeare's The Empire Striketh Back*. Let me lift the curtain a bit to tell you about four aspects of what you've just read.

First of all: what does Yoda sound like in a galaxy filled with Elizabethan speech? This was the question that gnawed at me as I began to write this second *Star Wars* book. Yoda is famous for his inverted phrase order, but many people who read *William Shakespeare's Star Wars* commented that every character in it sounds a little like Yoda. So what to do? Originally, I had four different ideas:

- Do a complete reversal and have Yoda talk like a modern person: "Stop it. Don't try, just either do it or don't do it. Seriously."
- Have Yoda talk in something like Old English, approximating Chaucer: "Nee, do ye nae trie, aber due it oder due it not." (My Chaucer admittedly isn't great.)
- Don't do anything special, and have Yoda talk like the other characters.
- Repeat Yoda's lines verbatim from the movie, nodding to the fact that Yoda already sounds a little Shakespearean.

In the end, as you've read, I had a fifth idea, which I hope was better than any of these. Yoda is a wise teacher, almost like a *sensei*—he has something of an eastern sensibility about him. Why not express that by making all of his lines haiku? Yes, I know: Shakespeare never wrote in haiku. But he did break from iambic pentameter in certain cases—Puck from *A Midsummer Night's Dream* speaks in iambic tetrameter, songs in several Shakespearean works break meter, and so on. And yes, I know: the five–seven–five syllable pattern I adhere to in Yoda's haiku is a modern constraint, not part of the original Japanese poetic form. Most haiku are simpler than Yoda's lines and do not express complete sentences as Yoda's haiku do—I know, I know! Remember, this isn't scholarship; it's fun. For you purists:

> If these haiku have offended,
> Think but this, and all is mended:
> That you have but slumber'd here
> While these haiku did appear . . .

Second, *William Shakespeare's The Empire Striketh Back* introduces us to the first character in my Shakespearean adaptations who speaks in prose rather than meter: Boba Fett. Shakespeare often used prose to separate the lower classes from the elite—kings spoke in iambic pentameter while porters and gravediggers spoke in prose. In writing *William Shakespeare's Star Wars,* I did not want to be accused of being lazy about writing iambic pentameter, but with this book it was time to introduce some prose. Who better to speak in base prose than the basest of bounty hunters?

Third, one criticism of *William Shakespeare's Star Wars* I heard several times—and took to heart—was that I overused the chorus to explain the action sequences. Some argued that I shouldn't have used a chorus at all, which I disagree with; when I began writing the first book, the chorus seemed like a logical way to "show" the action scenes without actually showing them, and there was precedent in Shakespeare's *Henry V.* However, by leaning heavily on the chorus, I neglected another Shakespearean device, of having a character describe action that the audience can't see. Here's an example from *Hamlet*, Act IV, scene 7, in which Gertrude describes what happened to Ophelia:

> There is a willow grows aslant a brook,
> That shows his hoar leaves in the glassy stream;
> There with fantastic garlands did she come
> Of crow-flowers, nettles, daisies, and long purples
> That liberal shepherds give a grosser name,
> But our cold maids do dead men's fingers call them:
> There, on the pendant boughs her coronet weeds
> Clambering to hang, an envious sliver broke;
> When down her weedy trophies and herself
> Fell in the weeping brook. Her clothes spread wide;
> And, mermaid-like, awhile they bore her up:
> Which time she chanted snatches of old tunes;
> As one incapable of her own distress,
> Or like a creature native and indued
> Unto that element: but long it could not be
> Till that her garments, heavy with their drink,
> Pull'd the poor wretch from her melodious lay
> To muddy death.

This device is called on more frequently in *William Shakespeare's The Empire Striketh Back*, giving the chorus a needed break.

Fourth, Lando. As much as I like Billy Dee Williams, and as smooth as he was in 1980, in my opinion his character isn't fleshed out very well. We never know what he was thinking when he was forced to betray his friend, or what made him decide to help Leia and Chewbacca in the end. Filling in some of Lando's story with asides and soliloquies that show how conflicted he feels hopefully gives him some depth and makes him even more compelling than in the movie.

Once again, writing *William Shakespeare's The Empire Striketh Back* was a delight. Most *Star Wars* fans agree that *Empire* is the best of the original trilogy, and I hope I've done it justice. I say "most *Star Wars* fans" because in fact, *Empire* is not my personal favorite. I prefer *Return of the Jedi*, thanks in large part to two things. First, it is the first *Star Wars* movie I saw in the theater (I was six). Second, when I was growing up we owned a VHS tape of *From Star Wars to Jedi: The Making of a Saga*, and I loved hearing about the seven puppeteers who made Jabba move, seeing how the rancor came to life, learning how the speeder bike sequences were done, and so on.

That said, of the three movies, *Empire* has the most Shakespearean themes—betrayal, love, battles, destiny, teachers, and pupils. All of those, plus the shocking father–son relationship. In some ways, *Empire* follows an ancient story form that Shakespeare used: a classic tragedy, with Luke Skywalker as the tragic hero. He is like the Greek tragic hero Oedipus, who learns only too late that his mother is his wife and tears out his eyes after she hangs herself. Luke discovers that Darth Vader is his father just after losing a hand—close enough, right? Luke also demonstrates some serious hubris, just like Oedipus: he faces Darth Vader before being truly ready, despite the objections of the two remaining Jedi in the entire galaxy. And he pays the tragic price for it. Along the way, Han Solo is put on ice and Leia's and Chewbacca's hearts are broken. All the heroes will, of course, live on, and the tragedy will turn toward Darth Vader's redemption in *Return of the Jedi*, but when you take *Empire* as a single unit, the tragedy is Luke's, and the rebels see the worst of things by far.

Thank you for continuing this adventure with me. I hope *William Shakespeare's The Empire Striketh Back* offers plenty for both *Star Wars* fans and Shakespeare fans to appreciate. For instance, I hope talking wampas, AT-ATs, and space slugs (to say nothing of singing Ugnaughts) bring a smile to your face. And did you notice whom Han and Leia sound like once they start getting romantic? (Hint: look at the line endings.)

The positive response to *William Shakespeare's Star Wars* was a gift to me as a writer; I hope my retelling of *Empire* (and *Return of the Jedi,* coming soon) is a fitting thank-you.

ACKNOWLEDGMENTS.

So many people provided love, support, and encouragement for the release of *William Shakespeare's Star Wars* and the writing of *William Shakespeare's The Empire Striketh Back* that this book would be twice as long if I tried to name them all.

Thank you to the amazing people at Quirk Books who make the *Shakespeare's Star Wars* world go round: Jason Rekulak and Rick Chillot (the best editors a guy could ask for), publicity manager extraordinaire Nicole De Jackmo, the epic Eric Smith, and everyone else at Quirk. Thank you to my agent, Adriann Ranta, for hearing every idea—even the crazy ones—and responding to them gracefully—even the crazy ones. Thanks to Jennifer Heddle at Lucasfilm and, once again, to incredible illustrator Nicolas Delort.

Unending thanks to my college professor and friend, Murray Biggs, who once again reviewed my manuscript to improve the Shakespearean elements of the book. He confessed to me, after reading *William Shakespeare's Star Wars*, that he has never seen the *Star Wars* movies but said, "I have a feeling about that Luke and Leia." I hope *Empire* hasn't crushed that romantic hope too harshly. (And wait until he reads *Jedi*—gasp!) Huge thanks are also due to my friend Josh Hicks, who has been my confidant for ideas about these books ever since I had the inspiration for *William Shakespeare's Star Wars*. Josh and I have spent endless hours watching and discussing the *Star Wars* movies (like all true geeks), and he has been a constant encouragement. Thank you, Josh—now let's finish that children's book.

My parents, Beth and Bob Doescher, are my biggest fans and let me know how proud they are every time I see them. I know how rare it is to have parents who love you deeply and let you know it, and I don't take it for granted. To my brother Erik Doescher, my aunt Holly

Havens, and my dear college friends Heidi Altman, Chris Martin, Naomi Walcott, and Ethan Youngerman: thank you for continuing to show your love and support as one turned to three.

I have been blessed throughout my life by wonderful teachers and mentors: Jane Bidwell, Betsy Deines, Doree Jarboe, Chris Knab, Bruce McDonald, Janice Morgan, and Larry Rothe top the list. Thank you all so, so much for the lessons in school and life.

A big thank-you to the *Star Wars* fans who embraced *William Shakespeare's Star Wars* (and me) so warmly. You are an amazing group of people. Special shout-out to the worldwide members of the 501st Legion, and especially the 501st's Cloud City Garrison in Portland, Oregon.

Thank you also to so many who offered their kindness and assistance: Audu Besmer, Travis Boeh, Chris Buehler, Erin Buehler, Nathan Buehler, Jeff and Caryl Creswell, Katie Downing, Ken Evers-Hood, Mark Fordice, Chris Frimoth, Alana Garrigues, Marian Hammond, Brian Heron, Jim and Nancy Hicks, Apricot and David Irving, Alexis Kaushansky, Rebecca Lessem, Andrea Martin, Joan and Grady Miller, Jim Moiso, Michael Morrill, Dave Nieuwstraten, Julia Rodriguez-O'Donnell, Scott Roehm, Tara Schuster, Ryan Wilmot, Ben Wire, and Sarah Woodburn.

Last but never least, thank you to my spouse, Jennifer Creswell, and our children, Liam and Graham. Jennifer continues to be incredibly encouraging, even though this endeavor has taken much of my time and energy. Liam stops everyone he can, even complete strangers, and tells them I am the author of *William Shakespeare's Star Wars*. Graham shows his support through the biggest, strongest hugs an eight-year-old can give, which are the best cure for just about anything. Thank you, Jennifer, Liam, and Graham: you are my high every day.

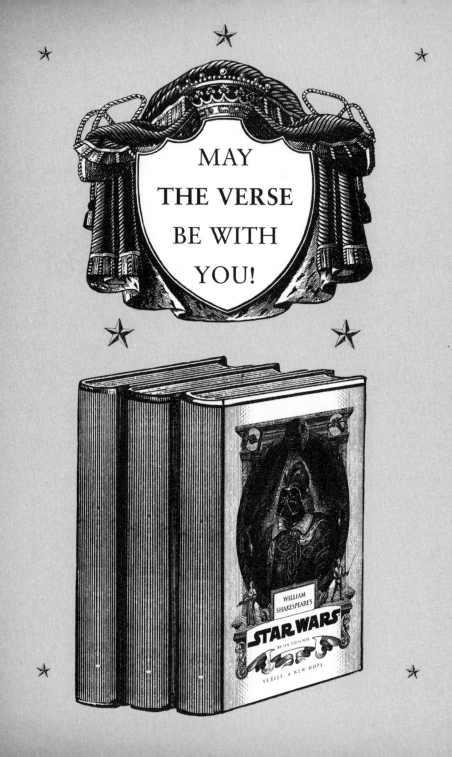

COLLECT
ALL THREE VOLUMES
IN THE
WILLIAM SHAKESPEARE'S
STAR WARS TRILOGY.

SONNET 3720-2-1
"To Thine Own Site Be True"

Thus far, with rough and all-unable Mac,
Our bending author hath pursu'd the flicks.
As thou hast read, the Empire hath struck back,
With grim Darth Vader up to his old tricks.
The tale is finish'd, but there is much more
That thou canst find within a website near:
A treasure trove of *Shakespeare's Star Wars* lore
From this book and the first that did appear:
A **trailer** for the world to share and see,
An **educator's guide** for those who learn,
An **interview** with author Ian D.—,
And **teasers** for *The Jedi Doth Return.*
As Hamlet to Ophelia did say,
"Get thee unto the Quirk Books site today!"

quirkbooks.com/empirestrikethback